Immersion

Stefan Budansew

CreateSpace

DBA of On-Demand Publishing, LLC.

All rights reserved; no part of this publication may be reproduced or transmitted by any means, electronic, mechanical, photocopying or otherwise without the prior permission of the author.

First published in Canada in 2015 by CreateSpace, a DBA of On-Demand Publishing, LLC.

Copyright © 2015 Stefan Budansew

Cover design by S.D.Budansew with images provided by NASA's Apollo12 crew, Nov. 1969 and images of the Perseid Meteor Shower, Aug. 18, 2014

ISBN: 1514158981
ISBN-13: 978-1514158982

stefanbudansew.wordpress.com

DEDICATION

For Peter Budansew, in memoriam.

CONTENTS

Acknowledgments	i
1	1
2	14
3	22
4	36
5	53
6	70
7	80
8	104
9	112
10	126
11	158
12	171
Preview of **Arktos** *Falling*	177

ACKNOWLEDGMENTS

I would like to thank Belinda Rees for her support and unwavering patience in helping me achieve my goals.

I would also like to thank Trudy Campbell and Nathan Budansew for their support in finishing the book. We shall always remember Chicago.

I would like to thank Heather Peterson for early inspirations which one day lead to what Immersion has become.

I would like to thank Sara Reller in providing the feedback and motivation to make this book a reality.

1

The breakthroughs on power generation came at the heels of the averted global war of 2015. War is always about hoarding and distribution of resource or security (perceived or real). Since 2009 the global supply for conventional petroleum peaked and the demand far out-stripped the supply and distribution chains leading to increasing global unrest.

Explorations in alternate power sources abounded - Solar, Wind, Tidal, Geothermal, Bio-Ethanol... all were too expensive or too limited in scope. Many scientists had given up on Fusion which has proven to be a dead-end for decades.

A radical refinement to the existing Polywell Fusor changed all of that - almost overnight. Upgrades and novel approaches corrected the limitations, allowing a sudden massive jump in efficiency. With this refinement, tritium was no longer required, and simple distilled water could be used to first generate the tritium required as part of the process.

Simple. Limitless. Power.

Realizing the far-reaching political and socio-economic impact of this discovery, the research team released their findings as publicly and as far and wide as possible. Science papers, internet forums, news sites - all were awash with the plans to produce the new Eagonston-Polywell Reactors (Eapos as they soon became commonly known).

Government backed by heavy oil interests attempted to suppress the information; however, world-wide universities, alternate power technical companies and even private citizens were building their own EAPO reactors.

The pressures caused by the oil crisis were starting to relax, and limitless power which was universally available was seen to be a cornerstone in ushering in a new era of humankind.

"Exploration of Shifts in the World Political Sphere"
- Prof. Wilheim Eagonston - 2016

The blast sent Adair flying twelve feet back through the air, the further 4 story drop behind him halted by the crumbling bricks forming a waist high lip around the edge of the roof. Moments later the 90 foot steel communications tower crashed down inches from where Adair laid prone, kicking up a blast of dust and metal debris. His raised arms protected his face - the hydrostatic gel in the braces, chest and legs solidifying to save him from the concussion of the blast. His dull tan urban camouflage armour took on a dusty coating while the blue UN band around his helmet was pitted and scratched.

Pushing a fallen cross-beam out of the way, Boyd stood up from behind the roof-top HVAC unit, a tired old monstrosity of steel which saved him from the impact of the tower, and made his way over to where Adair lay dazed. Large beefy arms reached down to first check Adair's vitals, and then under his arm to help lift him back to his feet.

"Next time... maybe how about we collapse the tower away from us?" Boyd quipped, reaching to lightly slap Adair's cheek. Adair's eyes rolled back down into focus. He coughed.

"Or better yet... use a timer. Or long string. You doing okay buddy?" His speaking was in hushed whispers, but jocular in tone.

"Yeah... next time..." coughed Adair as he practiced balancing on his own.

Following the void left by Boyd, Delilah crawled out from where she was pushed down. Seeing that Boyd was taking care of Adair, she raised her forearm and spoke in the same hushed whispers.

"This is Theta Sigma Team. We have achieved objective Pharos two..."

"I don't know why we don't just say 'we blew up the slotting communication tower'" Boyd walked over, still supporting Adair.

Delilah looked up from her wrist and shot a dirty look at Boyd. "We use code phrases in case the enemy is listening in. We don't want to give our objectives away."

Adair coughed again. "I'm pretty sure they noticed." Before them the 90 foot tower lay across the dilapidated rooftops, crushing through the top floor of the building next to them and raining debris down to the streets below. Around them sirens started to close in, and far off sporadic gunfire is heard.

"Speaking of noticed...we need to get out of here." Adair continued.

Delilah looked back at her wrist. "Theta Sigma Team... reporting in." She reached up to touch the side of her helmet out of reflex - as if the action could make the transceiver respond. "I don't think they are responding."

Adair frowns. "I'm pretty sure they would have noticed this too." he reaches out for Delilah's shoulder and tugs both towards the wreckage of the tower. "Let's continue someplace that isn't here."

"Woah... where are you going? What are you thinking?" Boyd resisted as they got to the edge of the building. Twelve stories below, a combination of military and police vehicles ringed the squat office tower which previously was the home of the tower.

"I'm thinking we jump this cheque before the waiter comes back looking for pay." Adair quipped and reached to test the stability of the girder which was spanning the road. It shifted slightly, but seemed to hold his weight.

"You have got to be out of your little mind!" Boyd protested as Adair took a firm grip and reached to start inching across the truss. He looked in despair to Delilah; however, she was watching Adair carefully before reaching to grip the truss herself.

"You are both certifiable."

Adair inched his way across, each step sending little dervishes of dust floating to the streets far below. As of yet the tiny figures making their way across the metal truss was lost in the mayhem below. About halfway across, the entire structure shifted, settling as a wall collapsed further. Adair's grip slipped for a moment and then caught. Glancing over he watched Delilah lean forward to hold onto the truss as it settled. The pair continued across.

Squeezing through the hole carved downward in the brick and wooden wall, Adair tapped a contact on his wrist. Nothing happened. Glancing down he noticed that the blast had shattered the interface on his braces. Reaching up he manually triggered the primitive pre-MESH local Comm-net.

"You should come over... I think your party is about to get company." Adair waved across the gap at Boyd, and then reached into a secured belt-pouch to start taking out a smaller charge of a similar nature that brought the tower down.

"Didn't have enough fireworks? Need to blow up this building too?" Delilah quipped, squeezing into the room. She reached up to join the Comm-net. "I think my entire Comm is fried"

Adair continued to work on the small putty-like explosives, attaching it to the sturdiest part of the truss structure. He didn't look up as he replied "I'm down to local-only. I think we're on our own"

The truss gave another shudder, and glancing out Boyd was seen clutching halfway across the structure. He shot the pair a dirty look before continuing.

"I don't know why I follow you guys... Adair, you're crazy, and Delilah you just encourage him." Noticing that Adair was out of detonators, he unclipped a small pencil-like detonator and handed it over. "Hey look - the welcoming committee."

Across the rooftops, soldiers carrying automatic rifles spilt onto the rooftop. Fanning out in military search fashion they started scouring the rooftop.

Adair finished, a little green light glowing on the tip of the detonator, and taking both Delilah and Boyd by the arms, he led them from the room, through a shattered door frame and into a dark cramped hallway. Studying the hallway, Adair counted the apartments on either side, and mentally finding the middle apartment he indicated a doorway. Boyd sighed, and then braced himself before shouldering through the door.

Wooden splinters from the doorjamb shot into the room as Boyd stumbled into the room. The contents of the room look like they were rummaged through and the inhabitants left in a hurry. Once upon a time lit by a single bulb in the room, the L-shaped room was both the living room and kitchen with a simple low-tech flat panel screen hanging skewed where it was knocked during the egress of the prior dwellers.

"Gee... this doesn't look like a staircase." Boyd quipped, as behind the group a dull WHUMP followed by the rending of metal, and crash of bricks, wood and glass to the streets below announced the detonation of the explosives.

"I'm pretty sure they will figure out where we went... they will be checking the staircases." Adair quickly went through the place, and into the kitchen. Pulling open the drawers under the sink, he started pulling out large pots left behind.

"OH...so you fancy yourself a bit of eating instead then?" joked Boyd.

Adair turned, crouched down and then started kicking at the wall inside the kitchen cabinet. Two kicks and the wood gave way. Turning he ducked his head in, before crawling completely inside. "Follow me" he called back.

"First I'm a tightrope walker... now you want me to be a rat?"

Delilah walked past, giving Boyd a reassuring pat on the shoulder, and crouching down, crawled into the space. She paused to turn the lights on her helmet on to reveal a cramped crawl space behind the kitchen sink. There was no floor.

"Watch your step." Adair was about eight feet below, bracing himself on both sides. From all sides rusty pipes of various sizes arched downward in an almost arrow-like fashion before ending in a twelve inch master drain. He continued to edge himself down the interior space, alternating between using pipes and the edges of floor joists to lower himself down.

"Oh...you have GOT to be kidding?" Boyd called out, and then started to wiggle his bulky torso into the tiny opening.

By the time they reached the ground floor, the group could hear soldiers searching the apartments. Orders were being shouted out in a foreign tongue - sounding vaguely Indian. The group continued climbing lower into the basement, and then squeezing as the master downpipe went through a hole in the foundation until the group found themselves in the access tunnels of the sewer systems.
"My Computer is down. Do you still have a map?" Adair asked in hushed whispers after he helped Delilah and Boyd through the opening. Boyd tapped his own wrist, calling up the inertial map.

Seeking the best direction along their route towards their final objective, the group picked their way carefully through the sewers. "I don't think I want to remember this." Delilah complained at last. "The tower was exciting, but this is just... vile". The group stopped at a ladder set into the concrete walls. Adair took the lead, crawling up and pushing the hinged cover open to crawl back out onto the streets.

They were about three blocks from the last tower, but the military presence was increasing and the group quickly hid down one of the narrow alleys between the haphazardly laid out buildings. "So... onto the primary target. A little more of Adair's magic," Boyd mimed an explosion with his hands, "and we can go home happy."

Adair paused and looked back. "No. We need to solve this in a different way."

Both Delilah and Boyd looked back curiously.

"Haven't you two figured out where we are... when it is?" Adair looked around, and finding a discarded newspaper he picked it up and folded it to present the date. The newspaper was filled with a curling script and faded pictures showing the exodus of the population. While they couldn't read the papers, Adair directed their attention to the Arabic numbers. 8 and 2015.

"Wait...August 2015... isn't that when..." Boyd started.

"Nukes. Yes... luckily the war had already evacuated a lot of the population, but millions died." Delilah was looking decidedly ill as the realization dawned. "I don't know why they would send us here for training. It's inhuman"

"We don't need to waste time thinking about that. We just need to achieve our objective and not blow ourselves up in the process." He crumpled the paper and the group continued working their way through alleys. Crossing a small court-yard, the group paused by a basket of laundry; fishing through it, they pulled out some large robes to drape over their military uniforms. Retrieving their Comm-net units, the helmets are left behind in the basket.

The group cautiously picked their way through the alleys following the map on Boyd's wrist, until it lead them to an open-air marketplace.

Although most people had evacuated, there were still dozens of peasants picking their way through the mostly empty stalls, seeking to purchase the necessities from the few vendors left behind. Most of the food and supplies appeared to be either locally grown or surplus UN aid resources which were being bartered and traded. Money took a backseat to canned goods, batteries and other survival essentials.

Delilah was first to spot their target. Loaded onto the back of a Tata 407 EX-2 flatbed was a small car-sized something hidden under a heavy canvas tarp. The truck was held up by a farmer who was leading a herd of large goats into the market. While it was not military, it was obvious that the people walking along side, and the motorcycle escorts were at least paramilitary in nature.

Adair studied the truck across the market, and then suddenly pulled both Delilah and Boyd behind a stall. "Did you notice that?" He hissed, pulling his hood back.

Boyd peeked out, and back. "What...the truck with the nuke on the back?"

"No. Look at the guns they are carrying."

Boyd and Delilah peeked out. The small carbines which were slung on the guards walking along-side and on the motorcycle outriders looked decidedly out of place. Sleek and brushed gunmetal black, the barrels were elongated wedge shaped which stopped at a tiny stubbed barrel- far too small for conventional firearms. A thin cord traced itself along the strap to a series of pouches containing the power sources - tiny chemical batteries.

"Puffers?" Boyd looked at Adair. "If we're in 2015, how can they have puffers?"

"They weren't invented until 2020… and it took a couple years before the Japanese let anyone else use them" Delilah added in a vaguely know-it-all sounding voice. "Those look like UN G-3's. What are you doing?"

Adair had retreated further into the shade provided by the tattered tarp overhead, and was removing his battle-dress. The hydrostatic-gel chest jacket and computer-embedded arm braces fell to the dust below. "Those puffers will rip right through this. I'd rather be nimble than dead." He pulled the robes back over his short, lithe frame.
"You can't out-run a flechette." Boyd pointed out sourly.

-- == == --

The dark cavernous room contained a series of sunken pits, and was bathed in a dim cobalt light. Each pit contained six high-tech chairs, each reclined back to look like a cross between a futuristic sacrificial altar and an autopsy table. Dark grey metal contoured underside folded along articulation joints allowing the table to morph its shape. The tops were covered with a padded surface containing an electro-chemical gel which provided cloud-like softness and full dispersal of weight across the entire platform.

On each of the reclined chairs laid one of the students of the United World Space Force Academy. The head-rest of each student gently wrapped under and around their heads, each containing a plethora of cutting edge 4GRE sensors and magnatomagraphic actuators to trigger REM atonia and provide computer controlled stimulus and feedback directly to the brains of the students.

Overlooking the still room was a smaller octagonal room suspended from the ceiling with angled one-way panels to observe the room. The man and the women in the room were dressed in smart grey and cobalt uniforms with their names over their left breast pockets. Beside them shimmered a projection of a shorter Asian woman, the holographic projection glowing a pale blue but showing detail down to the individual rendered strands of hair. She spoke with perfect non-accented English.

"Professor, you may want to look at this." She gestured towards one of the screens which switched to an overhead projection of the marketplace - the avatars for Adair, Boyd and Delilah clearly marked along with the target. Along the edge more details for the simulation streamed indicating everything from the various vital statistics for the cadets to the network environment stats.

The simulation zoomed in on the escorts surrounding the target.

"That doesn't make any sense. Those armaments are far outclassed for this time period. Elisha - has anyone tampered with the simulation?" The woman asked, stepping forward before being intercepted by the older professor.

"Wait - they are not in any danger. Let's see how they deal with this complication."

The hologram waited for a pause, before answering the question with a barely perceptible tone at the accusation "There has been no tampering with the simulation. I can find no edits to the source-files."

The woman frowned. "We've run this dozens of times in the past. And they didn't stack the deck against the cadets."

"Don't worry - we can run a diagnostic after the simulation has completed. Elisha, make sure you are recording detailed runtimes so we can fully pull them apart afterwards."

"Yes, Professor Sparling."

-- == == --

"So, what's your plan, Einstein? You just going to walk over there and rely on your charm and good looks to get them to turn over the nuke?" Delilah smirked.

Adair finished changing into the robes. "Hmm, no." he glanced over again and then back. "What if we removed the nuclear material, and detonated the priming charge. Could we not use it as an electromagnetic pinch." he mimes the motion with his fingers. "Pew... no more puffers?" Boyd watched on, bemused.

"You watch too many movies. A nuclear bomb is a complicated piece of equipment - it's not a tinker-toy set. "

Adair thought some more, and then pulled his hood up over his head. "Okay. I need you guys to cause a distraction. I'm going to circle around, wait for my signal and then poke the hornets nest with the sticks. I'm going to slip in while they are focusing on you."

"Oh... so now you're an action movie star?" Delilah scoffed. She considered, but couldn't come up with any other plans. "These objectives are ridiculous. We're out armed, outnumbered and are without backup. They are setting us up to fail."

Adair reached over to affectionately pat Delilah's cheek. "Yeah but they didn't bank on crazy." He ducked out of the stall and disappeared into the market.

Boyd nodded. "I know!" he exclaimed and crouched down over Adair's discarded battle-dress. Turning it over and searching through the pockets, he pulled out the remaining explosives. "Let's go cause some mayhem."

Delilah glanced out, not spotting Adair amongst the other cloaks, and then back to Boyd who was preparing the remaining explosives into little bundles with detonators.

"You're just as crazy as he is. You will both get us all killed." Pulling her hood over, "But I don't have any better ideas." The two left the stall, and entered the marketplace. They ducked between locals, making their way towards where the truck was stalled. The distance closed, and Delilah leant close to Boyd, whispering.

"Okay - so now what?"

Boyd glanced about, and then headed towards one of the stalls selling vegetables. The stall owner came to the front, speaking Hindu. Nodding and looking to the tables, Boyd lunged and kicked out the legs of the table. Mangos, tomatoes and okra fell to the dirt, and the stall owner launched himself at Boyd.

Delilah intercepted, grabbing the stall owner by the shoulders and twisting to toss him into the goat herder. The goats which were almost rounded up, scatter; many run to chase after the spilt food. The guards at the truck looked on, but with their training held their ground.

Adair had made his way around the perimeter of the marketplace, and was heading towards the truck. Trying to find an ideal vantage place to take on the truck and outriders, he looked up at the commotion started. "So much for waiting for a signal." he murmured under his breath. With most of the attention on the brewing fight between locals, Adair crossed the road and approached from the other side.

Gujarati joined in with Hindu as more of the merchants and buyers got involved into the fighting. Taking advantage of the Chaos, Boyd grabbed a passerby, and twisting, shoved him backwards into the guards.

The other guards immediately lowered their weapons as Boyd shouted an unintelligible mockery of their language, lunging forward barreling into the guard and reaches for the gauss carbine. Boyd grips the receiver of the carbine, and twists his elbow up to the face of the guard. The two bodies twist around as Boyd overbears and starts to get the advantage.

Another guard lifts his carbine to aim at Boyd only to be tackled from the side by Delilah. Whisper silent puffs from the barrel of the gun do no justice to the lethality of the weapon as a stream of dozens of metallic slivers, each with an atomic level thin tip of depleted uranium are propelled to hypersonic speeds and shot towards Boyd. The stream of darts silently chew up the dirt, hitting an unfortunate goat that was close to where Boyd and the guard were wrestling. Two of the goat's legs are cut in a red mist, and the bleating cry briefly overtook the crowd.

Taking advantage of the momentary distraction, Boyd yanked upwards on the gauss carbine receiver, catching the guard on the chin, then twisting around aimed the blunt square tip towards the cab of the truck before squeezing the trigger.

The windscreen spider-webbed and parts fell inwards as the door, the roof support, and the unfortunate driver were painted in a rough figure eight pattern of hypersonic flechettes. Panicking, the passenger bailed out providing the perfect opportunity.

Adair sprinted forward, catching the door of the 407 as it was swinging shut. Sliding across the broken glass, he shouldered the driver's torso against the mangled door ejecting his body onto the dirt below. Slamming the truck into gear, he ducked down as the windshield shattered and the roof tore into shreds as the outrider in front turned to fire at the truck hijacker.

Slamming his foot down on the accelerator, the truck jumped forward slamming into the motorcycle guard and shouldering him aside. It twisted sideways, avoiding most of the civilians and livestock in the street, shattering stalls and sending foodstuffs and textiles flying.

Seizing the opportunity of the confusion, Boyd finishes wrestling the gauss carbine from the guard, and tucking it under his robes he ducks into the crowd. Delilah follows suit, regrouping with Boyd at the far end of the market. Both look to the crowded narrow streets where the Tata 407 had disappeared.

The engine whined and the dashboard lit up with yellow, and then red warning indicators. Some of the errant flechettes must have passed through the engine compartment - enough to cripple the truck. The sounds of shouting and motorcycles were not far off behind him, and Adair knew he only had a few moments.

Remembering the map, he turned towards the Vivekenand bridge - racing towards the curved metal arching supports. Bracing himself as the Tata jumped the sidewalk, he dove through the empty doorway as the truck flipped the opposite direction, crashing first into the concrete bank, and then flipping forward into the Sabarmati river. Battered and scratched, Adair peered over the edge of the railing at the wreckage below, making sure that the nuke was damaged beyond all use.

2

Research students at Oxford University in the Experimental Radio Cosmology program were working on removing local system interference while studying the cosmic ray signatures of Quasars when a remarkable discovery was discovered. Repeating harmonics in multiphasic steps appeared too regular to be natural. After first ruling out man-made satellites, the interference was tracked to the Kuiper-Belt.

Copies of the signal were sent to other Radiography students, and a joint effort managed to decipher the signal. In addition to interlaced data signals, which were still unreadable, were video signals. Images of Earth, the science, military and political activities were intermixed with something... else.

While the 'Alien' images burst through the internet, every major scientific body denied and debunked and tried to discredit the discoveries as students went through archival radiographic data and found the underlying signal present for decades. Earth was being monitored, and it had been happening for as long as Earth was able to look back out into the stars.

Top level government officials began holding secret meetings with the Hegemony First Contact and Visitation teams. Meanwhile, worldwide tensions started to rise as the mania of 'Earth Invasion' and 'Government Conspiracies' started to grip the populous.

In the Hegemony Visitation and Monitoring forces, panic was also spreading. Their mission profile was in jeopardy despite all of their precautions; it was finally decided to make contact, and a single V&M ship was dispatched to

Earth.

Contact.

No lights from above - no large saucers hanging over capitol buildings. First contact is in an email to the United Nations Chairperson from the Hegemony V&M Contact ship. A meeting is set up on a remote Geneva mountaintop with U.N. Council Permanent members along with heads of state for the United States of America, Germany, Japan, the United Kingdom, France and India.

Scant information is released at first as high-level diplomatic talks continue with Hegemonic forces for several months. The world is plagued with UFO sightings, abductions, so-called 'true stories' and conspiracies of government cover-up. On November 1st, 2021 the United Nations gives formal world-wide notice of contact with non-human intelligences.

Global reaction is varied. Fundamental religious sects denounce the news and isolationist-leaning governments claim the news is western propaganda designed to influence their people. Relations between the major western countries and other large global powers who were not invited to the initial meetings with the Hegemony (Primarily China and Russia) suffer due to claims that the United States and United Kingdom were blocking and preventing their involvement with the negotiations. In the western world the benefits of technology exchange is felt almost overnight.

"*Contact - Loss of Human Innocence*"
Dr. Steven Hollister - TED talks - 2022

The lights in the Immersion Chamber stayed dim to avoid straining the eyes of waking cadets, while overhead the teachers and computer monitored their status.

Adair felt the familiar unnerving sensation as his brain switched to using his eyes and ears for stimulus. Opening pale bright blue eyes, he sat upwards, the contoured chair morphing and folding back upright as his back and legs shifted. He was shorter than most average cadets and while he wasn't the youngest cadet, he had baby-face features with a narrow pointed chin and small lithe shoulders and torso. While he may be short, he held himself with confidence and certainty.

On the chair beside Adair, Delilah was also coming to her senses, reaching up to hold her fire-red hair - not nearly as long as it was inside the simulation. Inside, one took on the mental self-image of how the psyche viewed itself - outside her hair was kept in a short bob due to regulations. She was tall and fit with a large, but attractive nose and an almost ruddy smooth complexion. She was dressed in the same unisex grey and cobalt uniform, with the name badge Telford. "I think someone needs to wake Boyd." She smirked at Adair.

The lounger with the large burly southerner, was still prone. Whereas Adair and Delilah have standard uniforms, the commissary had to special order a uniform wide enough for his shoulders. His dark hair was cropped close to his head, and his nostrils flared as he breathed deeply. The last one to raise, the chair itself started to shift back into a seated configuration as his brown eyes opened, and he stretched his arms wide - almost long enough to reach the chairs on each side. "Waking up is always such work"

The rest of the cadets were standing and stretching, conversations were quiet and in small groups as the lights were slowly brought back up.

-- == == --

The classroom was clam-shaped and tiered with each student at their own curving desk - slightly angled so everyone had clear view of the podium and curved display surface projected above the professor. Over their desks projected displays copying those behind the teacher, and the surface of the curved black surface was backlit with a myriad of keys and controls.

The display right now held several views of different cadet teams. Most were discretely infiltrating the communications arrays and achieving their goals with a varying level of success.

"Stop there. Focus on Theta Sigma." The professor didn't require any sort of microphone - his natural voice projected and filled the room. The screens coalesced into one master display. A loud explosion shook the virtual camera, and the tower crashed down, crushing the top floor of the adjacent building.

"How was the assignment worded?" The professor narrated sarcastically, "Covertly disable the enemy communication grid in your designated area."

On the screen the little figures inched their way across the crippled tower, disappearing into the building as the responding forces swarmed onto the rooftop.

"I think Cadet Fox and his team have a different definition of covert than the rest of us." A second explosion took out another half floor of the apartment cutting off the tip of the tower and sending it crashing into the respondent cars and soldiers below.

"Elisha, forward to primary objective. Focus on Theta Sigma" The action blurred as the camera shifted and panned towards the marketplace - the action sped up as time jumped forward. A small truck surrounded by glowing red targets slowly picked their way through the streets, stopping and stalled by the marketplace.

The camera focused closer as the altercation started in the market, quickly escalating until Adair jumped from the alley, hijacking the truck and driving erratically out of the market. The viewpoint followed the truck as it lurched through the streets billowing smoke until it twisted sideways throwing itself off the bridge.

"Cadet Fox. Cadet Johnson. Cadet Telford." The instructor called out, and waited while Adair, Boyd and Delilah stood up. The lighting in the classroom shifted, not-quite spotlights brightened up overtop the three cubical stations.

"I don't suppose you have anything to say about your actions?" The professor asked, expecting the question to be rhetorical.

Boyd and Delilah stood in silence. They weren't about to make matters worse than they already were.

"Sir. My team completed all objectives. We were not I.D.'d by the target forces. Most civilians had already been evacuated and the sabotage to the target infrastructure would not be easily undone."

"Where did you get those explosives, Cadet Fox? No-where did it say 'blow up the communications array'"

"Sir. Nowhere did it say not to blow up the array. We liberated the explosives from local forces."

"Cadet Fox - no one likes a smart ass. See me in my office after class."

"Yes Sir."

Boyd who had been silent up to that point couldn't hold it in anymore. "The simulation wasn't fair! They had puffers. There isn't any way they should have had puffers... the computer cheated."

The professor turned to face Boyd. "And do you expect that you will always have full intel on the situation at hand? That the mission will always follow your expectations?"

"No Sir! I do not place that much faith in military intelligence. It is an oxymor..." The class started to snicker along with Boyd's comment

"That's enough Cadet Johnson. See me after class." The professor stared Boyd down - daring him to continue. "And what about you, Cadet Telford? Do you want to join your friends?"

Delilah just stood silently, mentally cursing Adair and Boyd for taking a bad situation and making it worse.

"Well, at least one of you has some sense. Now, let's move on to Delta Epsilon - who didn't feel the need to make a simple exercise into an action movie."

-- == == --

Outside the Spanish sun bore down on the white stone buildings of the academy. Birds circled overhead and a group of the 1st year students were out in the grass expanse leading towards the dorm buildings having an impromptu game of football.

Delilah leaned against the cobalt tinted glass of the wall on the 2nd floor of the administration complex C2. She gazed down at the carefree nature of the other students, again wondering why her friends seemed to rather getting dressed down by the professors and not just being like other students. But knowing if they were like other students - they wouldn't be themselves.

The door slid open, and Adair and Boyd entered the hallway with the expression of scolded puppies. Delilah took one look at them and felt a slight regret at her thoughts moments before. Just a slight, though.

"Well... I thought that was totally unnecessary." Boyd complained "The game was unfair and we did everything. Half the teams didn't complete their primary objective."

Adair reaches up to pat his friend on the shoulder, and then swings his other arm around Delilah as they started down the hall. "It's behind us now - I think we should hit the Rec Center and leave this in the past."

Boyd seemed to shift his mood on a dime - which was contagious to the other two. "That sounds good. Besides...the decks stacked against us, and we still came through."

The three walked down the hall, crossing an arching glass encased walkway and cut through the classroom annex heading towards the Rec Center. Other cadets were in the hall as they passed.

"Hey Johnson... you sure showed us how brave you were crossing that tower!" One of the passing brunette cadets jeered.

"Hey...Johnson's not my name..." replied Boyd, before giving a lewd motion. "It's a description." The group of cadets giggled and continued on. Delilah reached around Adair to smack Boyd across the shoulder.

"You're a pig. No wonder you can't hook up with anyone." she rolled her eyes.

"Oh Delilah - you know you feel the same. You're just are afraid to admit it."

Delilah smirked as they entered the Rec Center. "Yeah, you're right. I would be afraid to admit I had a johnson like yours."

-- == == --

Adair sat at his desk, the surface split into several panes showing his ongoing research on his political ethics essay he was writing. On the wall in front of him more of his research streamed silently while the background showed a large autumn scene taken from back home - several thousand kilometers away.

"Adair" a soft completely accent-less voice gently spoke. "You have an incoming mesh from Delilah. Would you like to take it?"

Adair looked up from his work. His right hand was on a virtual chord keyboard, while his left reached out to flick between pages of his research. "Yes please." He continued to type absently with his right hand as he looked at the pane opening. Delilah was in a room mirroring Adair's.

"You know how Boyd was complaining about the game not being fair?"

"Yeah. And we got in trouble for that."

"I think Boyd was right."

Adair smirked "Don't tell him that. His opinion of himself is grand enough without us helping."

"I'm being serious. I reviewed all of the footage from the other teams."

Adair stopped typing and looked into Delilah's green eyes. "I thought the recordings were locked - we could only look at our own."

"Yeah... never mind that. Guess what I found?" Delilah made a couple motions on her desktop and Adair received the confirmation request for the file transfer. Reaching up to accept the files, he looked down.

Still images of each of the primary targets flashed up - one after the other.

"What do you see?" Delilah asked.

Adair looked between the images, using his hand to flick and go through the teams. "None of the other groups had puffers. They were all just standard. In fact Alpha team didn't even have outriders."

"Exactly. The game was stacked against us. And the professors are in on it. I interrogated Elisha, and there was no modifications to the simulation file. It was planned out this way."

"How exactly did you interrogate Elisha?"

"Adair! You're not focusing on the important part. Someone is trying to make you fail. Do you think it's Professor Sparling?"

"I don't know. But you can't say anything about this. They'd just claim we fabricated the evidence...it's our word against theirs, and they run the school."

"We gotta tell somebody!"

"No. We just gotta play their game. They hold all the cards right now."

Delilah frowned, and then disconnected without saying bye.

3

Modern space flight was not any one sudden inspiration, but a series of evolution, revolution and sometimes outright thievery of technology. There isn't any doubt that the technological exchange with the Hegemony did not accelerate the pace of human innovation; however, the fundamental foundation for spaceflight started in the 1950's with the first Space Race.

While it is good in theory to consider the United World Space Force as representing humankind in space, one cannot ignore the extensive forces also fielded under the United States Space Command and the Chinese National Space Program, and the vast independent corporate and civilian ships.

Space Stations and other installations slowly spreading throughout the solar system also benefited from the evolution of technology. There is also a growing social evolution of humankind leaving the old barriers behind; first with the independence of Armstrong Base, followed by Cyril Base, there was a growing trend to view humankind as one.

"Out of the Cradle - Space Technology Innovation"
— Sir Leith Telford II, D.Sc.h.c. - 2029

—

Delilah quickly crossed the academy grounds, ducking under the protection offered by the tall stone column supported overhang of the Rec Hall. A mid-autumn shower pulled the heat of the normally scorching Spanish weather into something a bit more enjoyable to those not used to the hotter climates, but it soaked the grey-cobalt uniforms. Inside, the Rec Hall was crowded with hundreds of cadets - most of the tables were filled up with people sitting on the edges of tables, or hanging over the edges of the four spread out holo-displays watching the activities.

The holo-displays were large, over fifteen feet to the side and had space on each side for five people to play. Three of these were displaying a popular space-sim with the group divided between teams and independent players each with conflicting goals. Their colour-coded ships sparkled and danced in the air in a symphony of physics and pixels.

The third table displayed a large complex field of battle - a large battle complete with planes flying overhead and battalions of holographic soldiers marched across the fields in a re-creation of one of the Sinu-Russian conflicts of 2014.

The perimeter of the Rec Hall contained a variety of canteens catering to different tastes of the cadet population. Strong smells from the coffee shop competed with cuisines from a rotating cadre of tastes. Today included Italian, Chinese, Indian and Mexican inspired dishes. Pausing to pick up a coffee in a 100% organic foamed pulp cup (to keep one's hand cool) Delilah studied the room, and then headed up to the 2nd story balcony overlooking the main room below.

The second story contained more transient food selections - quick snacking foods, as well as some tables better suited for quiet private group work with rounded tables and contoured formed chairs which were comfortable enough to sleep in. Several spread out view screens on the walls, not overlooking the crowds below, gave opportunities for study or entertainment to those groups.

Delilah found Boyd and Adair perched on one of the tall half-tables overlooking the groups below.

"You know it's not that..." Boyd was explaining. "They just don't want to face me again. They didn't like how I was able to take out their home base."

Adair smirked. "You took it out because I diverted their attention, and you kept elbowing both of the players on either side of you." he paused, carefully adjusting his tone not to hurt Boyd's feelings. "I've learned not to take the terminal beside you. I like my shoulders without yours in them."

Boyd turned and frowned. "It's not my fault they made them too small. And with all your flashy showing off, of course they all took after you. Leaving me clear to go for the win."

Adair didn't feel like pushing farther, and was thankful when Delilah joined their group. He shifted to the side. "Ooh...that smells good. You're wet." He pointed out the obvious.

"Yeah, it is. And it's raining out. Great observation." Delilah smirked.

"That's Adair for you." Boyd continued. "Small and likes to point out the obvious."

Adair reached over to playfully punch Boyd's shoulder.

"Yeah... whatever." Delilah was more impatient than usual. "Listen guys, I have something and I think you may want to check it out." She reached for both of their arms, pulling them away from the balcony. "Perfect for a rainy afternoon."

"You mean perfect for a rainy afternoon when you're procrastinating from writing your sociology paper you wanted me to help with last night?" Adair smirked.

"Hush you... just come on."

She led them away from the Rec Hall, taking one of the walkways to cut through the classroom annex on the way towards the Immersion chambers. Taking stairs down, the group left the classroom annex and cut through another open space to the squarish unwindowed Neuro-Educo-Physiology building. Smaller than most of the other buildings, and not build in the same Romanesque style which most of the academy buildings were designed, the N-E-P building had a rooftop of solar panels and a bank of vertical wind turbines to augment the Eapo generators for the massive power requirements.

Passing through automated security stations, the group enters the dimly lit Immersion chamber. A handful of the chairs were already in use, and the group quietly went to another section of the floor where they could activate their own chairs.

Delilah spoke quietly "Elisha, I need you to tie in 32, 34 and 38 into the sim. Please run from my personal folder the sim titled Archimedes- Avia class retrofit mk 0.8. Authorization Telford 2bk4 voiceprint Delilah Telford"

There was a momentary pause and the chair softly responded. "Acknowledged, Delilah. Voice print authenticated." There was a slight pause as supercomputers back in Scotland verified Delilah's authenticity to access the top security files. "Approved. Please lie back and relax."

Boyd and Adair just watched, their brows furrowed before moving to take the chairs to the front and beside Delilah. "What are you getting us into?" Boyd asked.

-- == == --

The universe unfolded and spread out before the trio. They were standing on a white platform which had several pedestals with computer controls glowing on a glossy black surface. The platform and computer floated... existed... hung in the air in the middle of a vast boundless plane of grey. An artificial boundary between ground and sky was delineated by a small shade differential in the grey.

Delilah walked over to the computer, placing her hand down and waited for the computer to unlock the files. A microsecond passed where her identity and authorization was confirmed, and then the platform and trio were joined.

The ship coalesced out of the aether before them. First at the speed of human sight, lines traced the major outlines of the ship. It looked vaguely like an upside-down shoe - the bulbous 'toe' hanging out in space and the heel wide and inverted. At the top of the aft portion of the ship nacelles formed with tiny forward facing twin engines which were dwarfed by the body of the ship. Fine details started to crystallize on the body of the ship. The lower section was the bulkiest, and contained a fly-through landing bay which had armadillo like blast doors to protect the wide landing bays - the front landing bay was fifteen feet tall while the rear bay was closer to thirty.

The entire vessel was around forty feet tall, and nearly two hundred long. The front had a 'flying deck' which jutted over a low-slung lower pod - the neck then narrowed before it spread into the main deck. The engineering deck spread out to nearly 80 feet wide before leading to the nacelle braces and contained the power systems, life support and the near technological magic of the FT-Hop drive.

Finer details started to emerge. Communication arrays, shielded x-ray lasers, spinal mounted coil-guns appeared as well as shielded rectangular ports and various cooling and thermal venting.

Colour started to spread over the surface - the ship was in the standard grey and cobalt blue livery of the United World Space Force. The ship's hull number and name came into being: SS/Da-02 AVIA DONAIR.

Boyd watched as the ship silently coalesced above them. "Avia Donair? What is that, a sort-of bird-meat? It's a dumb name for a ship."

Adair's observations weren't quite as childish. "I thought the naming convention for Archimedes class ships were all cities. You know... the SS Moscow... the SS Tokyo and SS Washington?"

Boyd turned "Dude, the Moscow was destroyed. My uncle was on it." He looked hurt that it was the first ship Adair brought up.

"Sorry Boyd. I didn't know that." He reached up to rest a hand on Boyd's shoulder.

"Not all ships are named after cities. The Archimedes..." Delilah started to correct Adair.

"That was the class ship - it doesn't count."

"So is this one. It's the class ship for the 2nd generation of Archimedes destroyers, besides there was also the Chuck Yeager."

They looked from the large ship to Delilah. "I've never heard of the Chuck Yeager. He was a famous American astronaut...wasn't he?" Adair asked.

"No, he was a famous test pilot. He was the first pilot to fly faster than sound. There is a top secret Archimedes technology test-ship called the Chuck Yeager. It's what we used to refine all of the advancements of the Avia class."

Their eyes narrowed further.

"What?" Delilah sounded a little taken aback. "I guess I've never really talked much about it, but my father's company... they are one of the major contractors for the UN. Telford Industries. They designed the Archimedes class, helped with the Galileo class, they even built about 60% of the ship - and all of the FT-Hop drive and avionics.

The boys looked back up, and started noticing subtle variations between this and the ships they grew up making model kits of, and in the countless video games they played - the ships which drove the dreams of boys to join the space force and go out into space themselves.

It was slightly smaller - more streamlined. The vehicle bay was also slightly smaller, but more aerodynamic and armoured. There were less weapons as well, but the lower profile would have greatly increased its in-atmosphere performance. Conversely, the engines and thermal cooling looked larger and more robust.

"So, you guys want a tour?"

-- == == --

Far away, and yet closer than any of humanity realized, hovered an entity. This was the opportunity it had waited for. Completely undetectable by the humans, Kh't L'nkt's consciousness floated in the cracks and crevices in the global-spanning MESH. By leaking the design and specifications, the D'rak N'li had also ensured that they would have free access to all of the information of the human species. Even not being a non-member of the Hegemony - the rules were clear. Humanity was open game.

What the D'rak N'li had not counted on was the paranoia of the human military complex. Even united by extra-terrestrial visitors, the world was still largely balkanized. Instead of one unified space exploration - three major powers vied for space supremacy while dozens of non-aligned non-governmental entities (the humans called them companies) would sometimes work to undermine globalization for their own advancement.

D'rak N'li was one of those trying to tip the balance, and his patience was about to come to fruition. Having thoroughly infiltrated the learning facilities of one of the factions (the one claiming to speak for the entire race, even while they only allowed selected balkanized countries to have influence in their actions), he was about to gain access to the technical schematics of one of the 2nd generation of the human exploration crafts.

With humanity on the cusp of settling outside their home system, and thus being eligible for joining the Hegemony, it was important to gain what information they could and either put a stop to or sabotage the humans.

-- == == --

The platform translated through the aether towards the landing bay. Delilah was at the controls while the boys just stood in awe. The silence was broken by the sound of the actuators engaging, locks releasing and the armadillo-like folds of the blast doors slowly unfolding in a ballet of machinery.

The landing bay was open to the width of the ship - minus the structure of the skin itself. It was nearly eighty feet by eighty feet, with the back half of the bay being about twelve feet taller than the front. In the middle was a large freight elevator with two smaller personnel elevators on either side. At the side of the bay, open grated stairs provided manual access to overhead catwalks and a windowed and pressure-locked landing bay control room.

The raised rear section was to handle the height of the two Tsiolkovsky class landing crafts. The Tsiolkovskys were larger than city buses and had side sliding egress panels on both sides to act as troop or cargo transport if required. A separate half-domed front section housed a control pod and a single HEPE overhead provided power to the two stubby extendable side wings. It looked like it had the aerodynamics of a brick married to a bumblebee- short stubby wings that looked ineffective, and a thick bulky rectangular body. It was only because of the techno-magic of the contra-gravitics and the High-Energy Plasmatic Engine which allowed the blunt-nosed craft to be single-stage to orbit.

The front section of the bay by contrast, did not require the height as the two craft there were short and angular - like modern jet fighters with chevron shaped wings. These one-person crafts were designed for one purpose - combat. The Sun Tzu Strike Craft were a mainstay of the United World Space Force. Armed with smaller copies of the capital ship's rail-cannon, they also carried two anti-ship MWPL Torpedoes - self guided weapons which would detonate and then use the explosive to generate a focused x-ray laser capable of cutting through most known vessels.

The platform came to rest in the center of the landing bay, and the trio stepped off. They had seen both the Sun Tzu and Tsiolkovskys before. They were more enthralled by just being there. Pausing to detach a sim-control from the panel, Delilah led the group towards the elevator. A circumference of blue outlining the door lit up just as the door opened. Stepping in, the group rode the elevator to the crew deck.

The crew deck was half taken up by the upper portion of the rear Tsiolkovsky bay. Hallways led back to the Landing bay control rooms, and forward to auxiliary life support. The rest of the interior housed bunk rooms and shower/change rooms, a blast partition separated the ammo and sundry storage which laid in open racks for easy access.

"Bah - I don't wanna see this. Let's go up to the bridge" Adair chimed, looking around at the grey walls before stepping back into the elevator. Up one more floor.

Unlike old style naval vessels, or popular science fiction designs, the bridge of the Avia Donair was in the center most protected part of the ship. Nestled beside the bridge was the main computer banks and backup life-support. Secured air-lock passageways lead aft towards more crew quarters, the ship's main mess and forward between the medical bay and the research labs, around the central bridge and past the ship's auditorium (a room for both briefing the staff, and used off-duty for entertainment purposes), and past primary life-support along the lower neck of the ship to terminate in one of the fire control spaces.

Above them on the upper deck the Captain and XO quarters and VIP guest quarters were at the fore of the ship near the main airlock while aft held the security bay on the way to the engineering deck. Life support and more fire control were also located there. Above that was a smaller deck which primarily consisted of upper engineering, communications and sensors, officer staterooms and primary life support. The front of the ship had a flying 'bridge' of manual fire control.

The air-lock door cycled opened soundlessly and the trio entered the bridge. The bridge was vaguely rectangular with the corners diagonal. Two exits framed the rear computer consoles and the center of the room was dominated by the command chair on a swivel. A small railing in front delineated the separation for the lower half of the bridge allowing the captain to easily look over the shoulders of the six other bridge officers (two to a side and two in front). Beyond them was the main view screen with one exit leading towards the fore hallways near life support, and the other leading directly into the Auditorium.

The panels glowed with displays - primarily white and blue hung ghost-like in the air in front of the panels with darker orange and red highlights on important read-outs. Boyd walked around the command chair and down the three steps to slide into one of the helm chairs - the electro-chemical gel instantly conforming to his broad body and bringing him close to the ebony-like display surface. Controls lit under his fingers and a display ghosted in front of him.

Adair moved to the command chair, slipping into the broader chair - the seat cushion tightening to support his smaller frame and make him somehow appear bigger. On his right hand a smaller curved panel extended from the arm of the chair with a smaller subset of controls.

Delilah hung near the door - she had seen this all on her own, and was enjoying watching Adair's and Boyd's reactions.

"Hey D… The computer is running diagnostics." Boyd spoke after examining his console. "I thought we were in a blank sim?"

Delilah's brow furrowed and she went to one of the rear panels to investigate, pushing the seat aside and standing as she stabbed quick commands into the interface. Adair spun the captain's chair around, leaning on one elbow to regard Delilah. Boyd stood up and climbed two steps, leaning on the banister.

Delilah ran diagnostics, her fingers a blur as she traced through the holographic display of the ship's internal MESH network. Orange trace lines danced and traced paths through the computers until they met at a central console. "It's up in engineering. C'mon.."

Taking the right front exit, Delilah dashed up the steep narrow staircase going upwards (faster than waiting for the elevator), her hands gripping the railing which was inset into the wall to help pull herself up to the upper deck, and then sprinted down the hall, following the angles of the hallway as they curved around the Captain's private board room and past the senior officer quarters before opening up into the security hub.

The central portion of the room held the secure armory as well as security stations while the walls were lined with smaller secure bunks - no privacy as the wall was made from transparent yet stronger than steel walls.

Running through heavily reinforced hatches into the engineering section, the two airlocks provided security by isolating the engineering deck from the rest of the ship, the group finally spilled into the aft-most section of the ship.

This room was easily the largest open space on the ship - or it gave the main hanger a run for it's money. Three massive High-Energy Plasmic Engines dominated the room with numerous access points and even more bulky mounting and controls which soared overhead - accessible in places by catwalks. Large machinery at both sides provided secondary plasmic channels towards the side nacelles to help with the contra-gravitics and the plasmic manifold which allowed the near physics-defying accelerations of the HEPE drive. At the head of each of the HEPE engines was an equally massive head-stone-like Eapo reactor. Two smaller Eapo reactors provided auxiliary power and allowed the ship's systems to be powered without the main drive being online. Several workstations were set along the interior wall, as well as at each of the massive HEPE drive cores.

Overhead a pair of narrow stair/ladders led up to an upper section where the FT-Hop drive machinery was located. The upper deck was dark, and there was no power going to the FT-Hop drive, or the HEPE engines. In fact there was no movement, no sound apart from one of the auxiliary Eapo reactors which was running.

Delilah went to the main engineering console, which was in the middle of running a full diagnostic. System by system, the complete specifications and running parameters were being checked, monitored, and logged. "What the heck?" Delilah asked, typing a couple commands, and then calling out. "Edia. This is Delilah Telford. Grant full access."

A melodious voice answered. "I'm sorry Delilah, I cannot do that. You do not have authority."

Delilah's voice lowered in tone. "Authorization Telford 2bk4 voiceprint Delilah Telford. Grant full access."

There is a pause, and the voice answers. "I'm sorry Delilah. MESH cannot be established with Telford Industries. You do not have authority."

Delilah frowned, lifting up her wrist to type commands into the simulation controller. There was a barely noticeable lag - which could only mean something was taxing the Immersion simulator to the point of causing a lag in the systems which should be working at near planck levels. Delilah muttered, not looking up. "Something is wrong here. I'm getting us out of here."

There is another pause, and suddenly the world went black.

-- == == --

Delilah was the first to sit up, faster than the Immersion chair could morph to adjust to her seated form. She reaches into her pocket, pulling out her pocket computer - one that was significantly more advanced looking than the more standard model which Boyd or Adair carried.

"Elisha - I need you to run a full diagnostics of the Immersion we were just in. Please display all tomographic telemetry information." She then motioned a few commands onto her own pad, holding it up as Elisha manifested a view-screen in front of where Delilah sat and started flickering through information. "Quicker - machine-read speeds."

Adair sat up, groaning. The strobe effect of the screens and data flashing faster than the human eye could comprehend did nothing to help. In front of him Boyd's table was still prone, and Boyd could be heard breathing deeply. He had fallen asleep again.

The rapid strobe of information suddenly stopped. Elisha spoke.

"I'm sorry Cadet Delilah. I'm unable to carry out your reply. There is no telemetry data recorded in my memory banks."

Delilah shot a smirk at Adair. "I figured something like that would happen." She pocketed her computer. "You remember the guns those guards had? I went back to review the footage. Except it wasn't there. It was accidentally lost during a data backup. The cluster was corrupted and was unrecoverable. In this day and age with the decentralized cell storage of the MESH - data was corrupted with no redundancies." she looked over to

Boyd, her tone lightening. "I can't believe he always falls asleep."

"If only you'd rest so much. Delilah - maybe there isn't a big conspiracy. Accidents happen, and the professors could just have been testing us" but he wasn't convinced - he just didn't want to openly discuss such things. Adair went over to rouse Boyd.

-- == == --

Adair and Boyd sat on Delilah's bed while she typed at a projected keyboard. The lights were dim in the room. Boyd kept looking over to the door - outside many of the other women in the dormitory waited, and he would rather be out there flirting than in here entertaining paranoid conspiracy theories. The school frowned on men being in the women's dorms - and it wasn't the first time Boyd would be ejected - and probably wouldn't be the last.

"There." Delilah explained at last. "Eden, access Sim telemetry. Please display the vitals for all participants logged in."

A different voice emanated from the holodisplay - her personal computer interfacing via the ubiquitous MESH. "Yes, Miss Telford"

"Miss Telford?" Adair asked as the holo display sprung to life with the respiratory, pulse, and a myriad of other traced factors. At the bottom of the display was a counter - 3 participants.

"I like my computers to show some respect." gloated Delilah. "So..there you go. That's all three of us."

"BORED!" Boyd cried out. "What's the point?" Adair gave him a playful slap, and then nodded for Delilah to continue.

Delilah rolled her eyes at Boyd, and turned back to her computer. "Eden - please display all synaptic activity on the simulation."

Three familiar graphs sprung into existence - ebbs and flows as the three of them went through exploring the ship; but curiously below was another line - this one was fainter, and scribbled at a magnitude looking like interference rather than a signal.

"What is that?" Adair asked, leaning forward.

"Eden - isolate the fourth signal. Remove the other signals, enhance and re-scale readout." The glowing patterns shifted - the 3 normal brain-waves disappearing and the last stretching and coming into focus as the scale of the display adjusted until the readout was more solid.

The readout danced far outside the range - not just human range but barely at the measurable extent of the computer which housed it. And it was present throughout the entire simulation.

"What is that? It has to be computer interference - some technical feedback."

"Feedback can't think. This is synaptic activity recorded by the simulation. Thinking."

"But no human thinks like that - it's barely inside the register."

Boyd leaned forward joining the discussion. "I think ... the computer has static... we're all lucky that the Space Police don't bust in here for us having access to that. It's security AIs... it's hackers. I think we count ourselves lucky that we're not kicked out of school."

Adair and Delilah looked at Boyd. Silence fell through the room. Suddenly the display goes blank.

"Eden" Delilah turned back to the computer. "Continue displaying the synaptic playback."

"I'm sorry Miss Telford, to which synaptic feedback are you referring?"

A stunned silence fell over the room. Not only was the school computer affected - not only was Elisha affected, but the influence also extended all the way to the private Telford servers - ones designed to house the most secret military advances of the United World Space Force.

"I don't think it's static." Adair said, his tone grave.

4

The collapse of the precursor to the modern MESH once called the Internet (also colloquially known as the web, the net, or a series of tubes) was almost inevitable after the surge of growth following the widespread adoption of Eapo reactors providing cheap, near limitless power without taxing petroleum resources. The growth was particularly quick and expansive in former 3rd world nations where the Internet provided a means to facilitate education, communication and the vast improvement of the human condition.

The source of the "Crash Net" virus (alternately known as Smoking Box, Powerout and Bengkul) was unknown but attributed to hacker-activists growing out of the group once known as Anonymous. Crash Net was able to spread through both mainframe and personal computers, through cell phones and even personal appliances and electronic toys. When it was attempted to be removed, the Crash Net would not only cause data loss, but it would also cause extensive irreparable damage to the hardware.

First looking like simple equipment malfunctions, by the time the virus was isolated and identified it had spread virulently throughout the world and in December of 2022 it is estimated that approximately 65% of all internet connected devices are infected.

Salvation came in the form of a joint Microsoft/Sun/Expanding Horizons venture to produce a replacement. With extensive Hegemony assistance, the joint companies rolled out the World-Mesh. Using simple, yet revolutionary design principles a scalable technological solution is rolled out and adopted worldwide. The proprietary software allowed limitless flexibility, providing an architecture that allowed software and data to be easily yet securely shared between personal devices and across worldwide distribution.

At the forefront of the technology, Expanding Horizons allowed Egypt to join the United States of America and Japan as the leaders in computer technology.

"From Tubes to a MESH"
— B. Marie Rees, BSE (CS) - 2025

"What did Professor Sparling have to say?" Boyd leaned closer over the table, his large nearly bald head sliding through the holographic display tracing light blue patterns across his face like some nouveau tattoo.

Delilah similarly leant closer. "Well, I don't have any proof. Not only that, I don't have any proof of not having proof. If we didn't all remember it - it would be like it didn't happen at all."

Adair didn't comment, his lip forming a thin line. This isn't the time or place to be having this discussion. He leans into the holodisplay to offer this opinion when the group is interrupted.

"I'm not interrupting you guys? Am I?"

Cadet Christina Grigg technically held the same standing as Adair; however, she had been at the academy a year longer and spoke with a firm authoritarian aire to match her formidable presence. Tall, shapely and with thick sandy blond hair (which was pulled back in a tiny ponytail - the extreme limit of the allowance for hair length) she was dressed in the same grey-cobalt blue uniform but seemed to fill out the role. She didn't wear the command stripes - she inhabited them.

"I know your little clique is tight, but our team needs to work together." she paused for effect. "As a team."

Adair shifted forward, redirecting his presence to defend Boyd and Delilah. "And don't worry - we will." He sat back, giving Boyd a gentle shove to allow the holo to reform.

"On the surface this looks pretty rudimentary. Multi-level complex with our goal at the lowest level."

More cadets came to join their little table as Adair continued to break down the objective. Before them the details were highlighted on the holodisplay by Delilah as Adair spoke.

"This top entry level - there are a couple choke-points. These split level entry halls have way too many access points to defend properly, and it should be easy for us to slip in. Besides the enemy would very much more likely be holding here and here - the hallways which lead to the escalators and elevators to the 3rd level. A small token force could hold back a much larger attacking force in these two access hallways.

The long hallways from both the first and second story which spanned over the side of the ravine ended in two small connected rooms allowing both elevator and escalator access to the third level.

I suspect most of the labs and storage on level three are just red herrings, but we don't know until we're on site and can MESH an inventory if there is something. Of course, if there is something in there worth getting - there will be someone in there trying to stop us. But the won't spread their forces too thin." Adair reached to gesture towards a similar choke point leading out of the third floor towards another escalator / elevator bay leading down to the fourth.

"This open central hall on the fourth floor is a definite killing-zone. Defenders can be stationed at the entry to all these halls on all sides, and we need to cross it to be able to access either of the staircases of the elevator going to the fifth floor. This is messy as there are several routes from four to five, and all of them in reasonable cover. It's much easier to assume that instead of spreading too thin, the defenders will pull and concentrate their final defenders on the key lab, down here on Fifth."

The screen continued down through the complex to the final room. Christina gave a mock clap. "So you were paying attention to the briefing. So it looks like a straightforward small-unit tactics Sim… with coordination between the teams. No need to blow everything up, right Fox?" The assembled cadets chuckled.

Adair thought. He knew something was up, and would not put it past the teachers to have a spy in their camp. Maybe it was part of the 'game' whoever was playing. He didn't intend to play by those rules. Glancing first to Boyd and to Delilah, he looked up at Christina who was still chuckling, and then dropped serious looking at Adair's expression.

"Christina… can we talk in private?"

A couple of the cadets gave a juvenile 'Wooo' as they parted, letting Adair walk away with Christina - his brown head barely coming up to her shoulders.

"What is it?" Christina crossed her arms across her chest once they were out of earshot. "I'm in command here, Adair. Don't you try to usurp that."

Adair's expression softened and he spoke quickly. "Do you want to win?"

"Of course."

"I think the teachers are cheating. Stacking the games against us."

"Yeah. I remember the puff guns. What did you want to talk in private?"

"I think they may have put a spy in our team."

Christina thought for a moment. "How do you know I'm not the spy."

"I don't. But I gotta trust somebody." Adair lied. He didn't trust her. He only trusted Boyd and Delilah at this point. "But if you don't know what I'm planning - then you don't need to trust me, and we can both win."

Christina weighted this in her mind, glancing at the expectant cadets. "Fine… I'm listening. What do you propose?"

"I'm going to switch the game in our favour. But I need you to look like you're playing by their rules. Front on - go full hard. You can even make it look like I went rogue when we start."

Christina nods. "Fine. You could MESH us for support." she offered.

"We won't be taking our MESH communicators - nothing that they could track us or detect us by."

"You're crazy, fox." Christina pointed out, her lips curling up in a smirk.

"So I've heard." Adair looked down, not returning the gaze.

Christina paused to place a hand on Adair's shoulder, giving it a momentary squeeze, and then in a more exaggerated gesture she pushed him back, raising her voice. "You talk stupid talk, Fox. You'll obey orders like everyone else, and don't you forget it." her eyes sought out Adair's but he didn't look back. Christina rejoined the group to plan the attack, with Adair returning after a moment pretending to sulk.

-- == == --

The cadets looked down, seeing their mental representation of themselves forming in the simulation. The whole team was dressed in United World Space Force Marine outfits, and were outfitted with a variety of gauss and hyper-kinetic assault weapons. They wore tiny ear communicators - transmitting full holo and biometric information via MESH to their wrist units. Outside of the large curving glass windows a fierce storm with hurricane-force winds and driving hail set the scene.

Christina stepped forward, in the simulation her hair long and flowing further enhancing her presence. "Okay, just like we discussed… but one change. Fox." she raised a finger and pointed.

"You and your friends - stay back here and guard the exit. That way you'll keep out of trouble." She sounded mocking and harsh. Tapping her ear, she added "We'll MESH you if you're needed. You won't be."

Turning she lead the group towards the upward stairs - deciding to take the upper story approach.

Boyd needed to be physically held back by Adair at the mocking. "That jealous two-faced witch."

"Hush Boyd - she had her reasons."

"Rear guard? This is a joke."

Delilah looked at Adair, and then a smirk came to her lips. "Yeah Boyd. A joke. Adair… this was all planned, wasn't it?"

Adair waited until the group had disappeared up the stairs and then reached to remove his ear communicator. "Take yours off too." he stripped off his jacket with the embedded MESH technology. "Jackets too" He left them in a pile near the entrance, looking over the weapons and after a moment, nodding and slinging his carbine slug-thrower.

Delilah and Boyd followed suit, and the group started towards the lower entrance, but then Adair directed them off to the side, heading towards one of the locked doors. "We can't trust anyone. I convinced Christina of that. We're on our own."

They walked up to the door, the embedded sensor scanning and then flashing a red indicator at the panel. "Delilah - I need you to bypass this." he looked at her apologetically. "Sorry that you can't use your computer either. We can't risk being traced."

Delilah looked back at the jacket with her wrist computer, but then reached and with Boyd's help to pry off the panel, started analyzing the optical circuits inside. Her delicate fingers worked, and the light hanging on the underside of the panel flicked from red to green, and the door slid open.

The group entered some administrative offices and Adair quickly went through several desks, searching. Delilah did the same, pocketing some small tools for later. Boyd stood a wary guard.

"Ah... this is what I was looking for." He held up a sleek wrist-computer. Tossing it over to Delilah he commented "Don't get too attached to it." and then lead them from the room, the long way across the open foyer and to an external exit. The new computer unlocked the door, and the trio braced themselves.

The wind made the rain and hail feel like needles as the group ducked outside, and covering their faces with their bare forearms, followed Adair around the perimeter of the building. The ground started to fall away into the ravine, and through the inclement weather the signs of a fire-fight on the long hallway of the first level leading towards the escalator could be seen.

Unnoticed by those inside, Adair led Boyd and Delilah to where the hallways left the building and started to hang over the ravine. About a hundred feet to the next building, and the ground fell away to a height of about fifty feet. Looking up at the repeating X-shaped braces of the underside of the hallway, Adair started to hand over hand.

"Oh you have GOT to be kidding me?" Boyd realized Adair's plan. "Did you NOTICE the hail Adair? You are crazy. CRAZY!"

Delilah slid up beside Boyd with a wild look in her eyes and a smile. "Crazy like a fox. C'mon Boyd - I like it when you show off." She started to follow Adair across the underside of the walkway.

"Oh MAN!" Boyd whined watching his friends. "It isn't so bad playing by the rules, y'know." His arms glistened from the rain as he stretched and followed.

The overhang thankfully provided some protection from the winds and rain, and while the metal was cold, the exertion compensated and at the far end, a small ledge ran around the tiny connecting building. Climbing up to the roof, Adair slipped over to the far side where the escalators lead downwards towards the next floor. The slope of the escalators followed the sides of the ravine, and the forty-five degree angle slide was slightly arched. The slightest miscalculation and one would fall off the building and down into the tree-hewn side of the ravine.

The rain made the metal roof slick, and Adair laid on his stomach and slide over the edge, his arms spread wide to hold the top panel of the dome. He slid down experimentally, stopping after a couple feet. The wind picked up threatening to throw him off the roof.

"That's why you didn't want cameras" Boyd complained. "If they thought your last Sim was risky and stupid... who knows what they'd call this." Adair didn't hear him - he was already sliding down the roof of the escalator.

"You go first Boyd." Delilah said, resecuring her tools and reaching to push her wet hair from her face. "That way you can catch me if I fall." She tried to give him a smile. Boyd just shook his head.

"You're as crazy as he is for following him." He laid down and followed Adairs lead, sliding and using his feet and hands to slow his descent.

"What does that make you?" Delilah asked rhetorically as she brought up the rear.

Delilah could barely keep her grip on the slick metal. Not having the grip-strength that Adair and Boyd had, the wind kept making her grip slip and her hands ached. She tried to estimate the distance, by looking up, but her bangs just blew into her eyes. She moved her body to try to glance downwards, and her left hand lost grip.

Fingers flailed to grab the edge, but she couldn't catch it, and started an uncontrolled slide down the escalator. She screamed by uncontrolled reflex.

Boyd looked up just in time to see Delilah sliding down - slowly sliding off the side of the arched roof.

"Oh damn it all." he cursed, shifting his weight down and digging his feet into the metal. Taking a deep breath, he released his grip with his hands shifting to prepare to catch Delilah and brace for the impact.

Delilah desperately tried not to fall sideways off the top. Time seemed to flow like syrup as her legs came into Boyd's reach. He pulled on her thighs, guiding her feet towards his shoulders and reached upwards towards her hips. Her weight came down into his body, and his feet edged forward, but did not lose their grip.

"Gotcha." Boyd exclaimed, his large hands tightly gripping Delilah's slick waist. He grunted as his body absorbed her motion.

Delilah panted for breath. She didn't move - didn't look back. "Thanks..." she breathed out. She slowly uncurled her feet from Boyd's shoulders and found purchase on the sides of the roof. Making sure she was safe, Boyd then continued the final distance to the roof. Adair was there at the bottom to help both of them stand up.

Delilah was bruised from her fall, and looked to Adair. "Maybe Boyd is right. This is crazy." she said softly - her spirits as bruised as her hands.

Adair gave Delilah a hug, joined by Boyd. "We're almost there. We can do it together."

Picking their way across the rooftop of the third level, Adair found a rooftop comm array and motioned Delilah over.

"Do a quick scan of what's on level three."

Huddling close to protect themselves from the biting rain, they looked down at the holographic display as Delilah accessed the buildings MESH network.

"I don't know Adair. I don't see much."

Adair studied the plans. "There. We can go there and sabotage the main electrical trunk. Turn off security - turn off the power."

"I can do that stuff remotely Adair." Delilah looked at him deadpan. "We don't need to go there."

"Could that be traced?"

"Hypothetically."

"Then no."

Boyd joined in. "What if you set a fuse?"

The two looked at him. Delilah spread into a smile. "I could set a timer. Tell me what you need, and we could let it happen."

Adair paused, going over details in his head. "Okay… this is what we need."

-- == == --

Professor Sparling leant over the displays, watching intently. His gaze was on one particular group - their glowing representations clearly outside the pattern of attack and defense being played out on the levels inside the complex. He dialed back the weather - even the near catastrophe didn't deter the group on their crazy plan.

Behind them, the door to the officers level opened, and the base commandant stride in accompanied by two others.

Vice Admiral Henry-Joseph Rees was the chief administrator of the school, however he left most of the day-to-day running of the operations to his instructors. With the global spanning recruitment and obligations, political machinations was where the Vice Admiral spent most of his time. A tall and severe looking man, Vice Admiral Rees was fiercely loyal and would defend his school and students at all costs. He was a long-time acquaintance of his one guest, his tall knife-like body in contrast to the shorter wider envoy.

Under-Secretary-General Kristoph Wakelin of the United World was the official envoy liaison between the United World government and the Hegemony Visitation and Monitoring High Command. He was a larger man, and was proud of his place and position. Originally a low-level research liaison, he was in the right place and the right time when the Hegemony first contact happened. A minor aide at those critical first meetings, he now had risen to the rank of Under-Secretary-General and represented the United World government (which in his mind meant by extension all of humanity) in negotiations with the Hegemony. Politically speaking that put him in a pivotal role. It was their guest who would have in normal company completely turned heads.

While aliens were known to be in existence for almost a decade, most of humanity had never seen an alien - apart from the carefully staged and edited television appearances.

Agiprom Prime Centri was typical of the Mara. He stood just over seven feet tall, and had broad almost insect-like shoulders and two sets of arms which were longer and slender compared to human. His face was bilaterally symmetrical, with elongated features and a head-crest which wrapped from side around the top of his head to the other side in the place where ears would be. He wore flowing white robes with intricate gold baubles hanging from his lower shoulders across his chest. He spoke not only English, but also over fifty human languages fluently. With his Mara implants could speak literally any language or communication method (machine, human or even advanced creature) on the planet.

Centri - like the rest of his race, was bio-genetically-engineered to interface with human-kind. He was alien enough to give a sense of awe and command respect, yet human enough to be relatable to. He was grown and developed and educated in the entire human experience in diplomacy and propaganda. He was on a mission.

"Esteemed Under-Secretary-General. This one again is grateful for the opportunity to see the future commanders of your burgeoning space fleet." USG Wakelin beamed - he always liked his one-on-one dealings with Centri - it always left him feeling important.

"Vice Admiral Rees. This one expresses gratitude for the opportunity to review your facilities. Perhaps you could explain the activities of these students?" Centri motioned with his upper arms at the slanted glass overlooking the prostate cadets below.

The Vice Admiral was not sold on this 'slick alien talker' bit. In his experience, the entire decade of exchange had been entirely at the whim of the Mara. They would share little of their own - little of the Hegemony. They hinted at the existence of other aliens, but handled all of the diplomacy and interactions solely through the Visitation and Monitoring team - solely through other Agiprom Prime Mara's. To Vice Admiral Rees they were little more than spin-doctors who were manipulating humanity for their own needs.

"Of course Agiprom Prime Centri. This is one of our Immersion Chambers. Students are involved in a training simulation. The Immersion Chambers allow us unlimited flexibility in setting up scenarios while also allowing us to monitor the reactions and responses of the cadets."

His upper arms folded across his chest, and his lower right arm reached out. "And what of these readings here." he indicated the three glowing symbols who were standing outside the main simulation - skirting around the set rules.

"Ah. Yes. Professor Sparling - perhaps you could provide your personal insight on those particular cadets."

-- == == --

Adair leaned back against the doorway. It wasn't like the standard pneumatic actuated doorways, but a physical maintenance hatch which he had to push closed using his shoulders against the winds outside. The indicators in the corner of the portal blinked red - the door was in maintenance mode. No alarms had been triggered.

Adair didn't bother with his light, using the little ambient light coming from small windows set high in the room along with the glowing indicators from the HVAC machinery. The large electric turbines drown out his footsteps as he walked into the room, leaving wet footprints behind him. His clothing was soaked and his hair matted to his face. He wondered if he could catch a cold - but this was ultimately - just a simulation.

A simulation of a cold then… he pondered as he slowly crossed the maintenance room. He approached the doorway, stepping to the side not to trigger the automatic door opening. Another part of his head was counting up slowly. Twenty seconds passed, and the door panel changed from a green glow to a flashing red. He stepped up, and reached to gently open the door by hand, sliding the door sideways.

The hallway wasn't meant for the public access - it was not as finished as the rest of the complex. The ceiling was a standard drop-tile and the florescent lights bare with no covers. Following his internal map, he turned down the hallway, pausing to glance around a corner and then followed until he reached another unmarked doorway.

Again pausing, he counted thirty-five seconds this time before the door switched to maintenance mode, before sliding the doorway open. He slipped into the plumbing machinery room, walking to the edge where the floor opened up to large water tanks for holding the fourth and fifth floor solar heated water. Climbing down a ladder, he found the appropriate access tunnel, and started climbing down the water supply and return pipes in the narrow space leading down to the fifth and final level.

Cramped and trying his best to avoid burning himself on the pipes, he heard the far off muffled sudden commotion. Shouting, and general confusion let him know that the next step of his plan had went into action. He still wasn't sure how Cadet Grigg and the rest of her team was doing, but that really didn't hold any bearing. Reaching the bottom, the maintenance room was nearly pitch black, and the door's indicator was already flashing red. He had no choice at this point but to use his flashlight. Turning it on and affixing it to the barrel of his gun, he slung the weapon in one arm while he gripped and shouldered the door open.

The lights were off in the corridors of the fifth level. Even the emergency lights had been by-passed, and the storm shuttered closed leaving the level in utter darkness. The hallway was well appointed - faux marble floor and the occasional standing potted plant or object d'art cast strange shadows. In both directions, the beams of flashlights could be seen as the defenders on this level struggled to regroup.

Adair headed away from the final objective, taking a circumventing route towards the goal. He paused when he heard the muffled tones of "Hell's Raining Down" by Tiramisu. That was Boyd's contribution to the plan - the MESH communication channels have been jammed in test mode, and the diagnostics files replaced by the popular electro-dearth-grunge pop song. It was also useful to let him know when he was getting close to defenders, allowing him to momentarily hide or turn off his flashlight to let the individuals or small groups pass.

Adair was close to the destination, and it seemed like everything was going smooth as teflon. His carbine was being held low, aimed forward to use the flashlight to navigate the maze of hallways. Turning a corner, a guard waiting with her light off turned it on suddenly and shined it up into Adair's face momentarily dazing him.

Adair reacted the same, shining his light up into the face of the person before him.

Time hung still. Before him was the most beautiful woman Adair had ever seen. Her shimmery black hair hung down past her shoulders in waves. Her wide stunning light brown eyes blinked and then stared back into Adairs. Her skin had a beautiful olive-tan to it, and her lips had a shy sensuality to them. She was utterly stunning.

Adair looked like a drowned rat. His hair was matted down, and the rain and sliding managed to scratch and dirty the supposed super-material of his uniform. There was no denying the coloured trim on his shoulder - his blue to her red. His Montague to her Capulet.

Neither one of them spoke, just staring at each other, both of their rifles at the half ready - neither one willing or able to make a move. A small quirky smile slowly came up to Adair's lips. After a moment of reflection, a small smile crept up onto her lips too, which seemed to light up her face. Adair felt his heart start to pump faster.

Adair realized that he had lost. There wasn't any way he could shoot this woman. Slowly, he lowered his gun. A frozen moment later, she lowered hers. The mexican stand-off continued.

"Hi." Adair managed to find. Instantly he thought how terrible that was for an opening line. This wasn't a place for lines in any respect.

"Hi." She answered shyly back. Her voice was a soft and beautiful as her appearance.

Adair was about to continue when their monosyllabic exchange was interrupted. Down the hall a patrolling set of red defenders approached. Adair managed to tear his eyes away for a moment, glancing down the hallway, and back. When he looked back she was still regarding him.

"Go." She said.

Adair lingered as long as he could, before the point of no return. "Bye." he said, and then retreated back the way he came, turning off his light and recklessly dashing in the pitch black. Behind him he heard the exchange.

"Hey Lil - Nathan seems to think that this is a trick. They may be trying to sneak past and infiltrate. We're going to guard access to the lab."

Lil… so that was her name. Adair ran head-long into the wall in a twist of the hallways, dazing himself for a moment. Stars danced in front of his eyes. 'What just happened?' he thought to himself. 'I've never gone all moon-eyed over a girl before.' He was staggered and exhilarated and embarrassed all at once.

Gunfire brought him out of his reverie. The fighting was getting closer, and now there was additional guards on the lab. A simple trigger pull, and he would have been in, but that was something that was impossible for him.

He looked around, and then looked up.

Shouldering the rifle, Adair climbed one of the statuary and pushed the plastic and foam acoustic ceiling tile aside. Reaching up, he took one of the braces for the drop ceiling and pulled himself up. Flattening himself against the small crawl space between the building's superstructure and the suspended frame for the ceiling, he replaced the missing tile, and then started crawling down the hallway.

The metal brackets had flanges which cut at his hands and shredded his knees, but Adair crawled in silence. He was late and the final stage of his plan was about to start. He would not be in position.

He heard a sudden cry all around underneath him as the lights suddenly returned - in full intensity. Suddenly the crawl-space lit up with little echos of light sneaking up between the edges of the tiles. Below he heard the confusion as everyone was dazed by the return to light. The distraction wouldn't last long. He should have been in the lab able to do the final download once the computers rebooted. Instead he was dozens of feet away reduced to a slow crawl - literally.

The last thirty feet seemed to take forever, but he finally estimated that he was over his target. He listened carefully, but didn't hear any sounds. Reaching down, he lifted a ceiling tile out of the way, and then started to lower himself down.

A blur of motion, and Adair suddenly found himself pulled from the ceiling, his small frame crashing down into a desk as strong arms wrapped around him. He wiggled, jabbing upwards blindly where his assailant's throat would be and twisting to break the fall.

Boyd staggered back, only his frame and reflexes saving him from being incapacitated.

"FOX!" he hissed as Adair rolled into a combat stance. "Holy Pope on a Rope!" A hand reached up to hold his throat. "I'm lucky you're such a bad scrapper."

"You're late. So much for your plan." Delilah snarked from the computer where she was working. "You look like hell."

"What are you two doing here?" Adair finally was able to ask.

"D's idea. We're the backup to your plan. Good thing too." Boyd smirked.

"Yeah... Boyd... while you're busy gloating how we got one up on Adair - you mind going back and watching the door?" Delilah motioned towards the door where two cadets with red uniforms were crumpled unconscious. She lowered her head and continued at the terminal.

Adair came over. Delilah spoke without looking up. "I don't know how you were planning on getting the data - not without any MESH computer." On the computer table was one which was obviously from one of the fallen defenders - based on it's red trim. The data transfer was nearly complete.

"I'd have improvised." Adair said.

"This is easily." Boyd commented from the door. "It's like the guards just walked away and let us in here." That prickled the hair on the back of Adair's neck.

"We gotta go."

"I've not erased their storage yet."

Adair reached to the computer in front of Delilah and took the computer, attaching it to his wrist. "Now."

Adair took Delilah's arm and dragged her towards the door.

"It's still quiet out there." Boyd commented.

"That's what I don't like."Adair replied, leading the group out down the hall and back towards the mechanical room. The sound of gunfire was closing - apparently Christina wasn't doing too bad leading her forces on a final push.

Rounding a corner, the trio closed on their exit strategy. The door to the mechanical room was feet away. Hearing fighting close-by the group ducked into the mechanical room.

It was a trap.

The room was filled with red-trimmed defenders. Boyd stopped immediately, and was almost walked into by Adair and Delilah. The three raised their hands.

"Well... sorry to interrupt your party. If you don't mind... we'll be on our way." Boyd quipped as the group - equally startled raised their guns higher. Adair and his team dropped their carbines to the floor.

Cadel Trevor Duffield - McDuff to his friends - was the leader of the defenders and here in person. He picked his way through the defender, raising a hand to touch the shoulder of the attractive defender Adair ran into previously, and then approached Adair, his hand outstretched.

"Awww... hell" Boyd explained as Adair removed the wrist computer and dropped it into McDuff's hand.

"Thank you. Now if you'll turn around and make this easy for us... this was a no-prisoners mission."

Delilah didn't say a word, raising her hands to behind her head and turning away from the defenders. Boyd continued to murmur expletives as he did the same. Adair looked up, meeting the eyes of the unknown defender. She couldn't hold his gaze, looking down at the ground.

McDuff stepped between them, giving a prodding nod to Adair. Adair assumed the position, hoping for a last-minute rescue from Griggs, or for the lights to go out, or any number of completely random things to turn the tables. For some deux-ex machina to save them.

The sound of gunfire cut off the expectations.

-- == == --

Agiprom Prime Centri unfolded both sets of arms as he watched the simulation. His bony ridge twitched but gave away no indication of his thoughts as he watched the defenders suddenly and inexplicably pull back most of their forces to an empty mechanical room near the target. A skeletal defense force was left to deal with the main attacking force.

It was if they were psychic - the ambush perfectly stopping what was an otherwise perfect end-run.

"Fascinating. This has been most illuminating. Under-Secretary-General - perhaps we can continue our tour."

5

Contact between the Hegemony and humankind existed on several levels.

Official contact between the Hegemony Visitation and Monitoring teams was always conducted by the Agiprom Prime who were always of the Mara race. That was the only official race who could deal directly in any official capacity with the world governments. Every major country had their own assigned Agiprom Prime and were all treated equally and with distant arms-length diplomacy.

On the unofficial level is where things were more messy. Working through human intermediaries and remote drops, other factions within the Hegemony worked with private human interests. Sometimes in exchange for precious metals, or for future considerations humankind was able to gain more fruitful technological wonders through these illegal means. From new illicit drugs, bio-psychoactive compounds, to MESH and Eapo refinements, to the FT-Hop drive itself. All were seeded through illegal dealings with the D'rak N'li, the Hoo'lou'loon, the Xqyumm and dozens more.

It is quickly apparent that within the Hegemony itself, there are stratified layers, and complicated nuances which mankind is not privy to knowing. The Mara presented a unified front for the Hegemony, but when the separate pieces were put together, the true full picture was far more complex with competing agendas.

excerpt, "UWSF report on Hegemony Order"

— *Secretary-General Walter Schenck, 2029*

Adair stared off over the edge of the balcony at the cadets collected below. His coffee sat cooling on the small table before him - untouched. Boyd and Delilah also sat at the table, arguing.

"And you know this for certain?" Delilah was skeptical

"I heard it from Dave who heard it from that short little indian guy - whats-his-name Akshat. Who heard it from McDuff himself. They were in the middle of a firefight when the computer told McDuff to send forces to the mechanical room."

Delilah's first reaction is to bring up her wrist-comp. Boyd reached to take her arm, intercepting the motion. "Don't both. Elisha has no records of it. She also indicates it would be against the rules for her to directly influence the simulation."

"Just like it's against the rules for the defenders in the 2015s to have puffers." She reaches to nudge Adair. "Hear this, fox?"

"So of course I go to Professor Sparling. And he's even more surly than normal. I barely got out of there without a detention."

"I think I know why that is. Emma was saying that there were some major UW people here, including one of the alien caretakers."

"Caretakers?" Boyd looked confused at the term.

"You know - those liaison officers. The tall creepy looking ones with the four arms who are supposed to be our bastions of advancement."

"Why would one be here? Hey Adair?" Boyd reached over and nudged Adair. "You're quiet... you should be all upset about this. Or even listening."

Adair was pulled back to the table. "Eh? Upset. No." His gaze still wasn't present.
Delilah and Boyd had never seen Adair behave like this before. Glancing at each other, Delilah moved behind him, reaching to take and pin his arms

back as Boyd came close.

"Adair, buddy. I think you're going to have to start sharing. Inquiring friends are concerned... it looks like you left your mind back in the sim."

Adair struggled, but didn't want to overtly cause a scene. He exhaled.

"In the sim yesterday..."

"Yeah, we we talking about that. They cheated again." Boyd leaned closer, grabbing the first thing at hand - Adair's coffee - as something to mock threaten with.

"No, 'not that. In the sim yesterday." He exhaled. If he couldn't tell his friends... "Before I downloaded the file."

Delilah chimed in over his shoulder. "We downloaded the file - you were late."

Adair continued, ignoring the baiting. "I ran into a cadet. One of the reds."

Boyd smirked, still holding the coffee. "So you were sloppy. I always think you shouldn't bother going off. I'm much better at this infiltration stuff than you are."

"I couldn't shoot her." Adair exhaled and looked down.

Delilah processed this, and as the realization dawned on her, she released the grip on Adair's arm. She came to the side with a sympathetic and slightly curious look in her eyes.

Boyd still didn't catch the nuances. "What? Big deal. So you suck at shooting too. Wait - you didn't shoot her... so she's the one who ran off and warned McDuff?"

Adair nodded - assuming it to be true. Assuming he was the one who ruined everything.

"No Boyd. You said that Dave said that Akshat said that McDuff heard it from the Elisha."

"Then what is the big deal?"

Delilah looked over with a broad smile. "Gawd you are so thick." She moved to the edge of the railing on the other side of Adair. "So, where is she?"

Adair shrugs his shoulders. "I don't know. I don't even know her name."

Boyd was getting frustrated. "What is the big slotting deal? Delilah - why are you smiling. He screwed us over?" The cold coffee was being spilt as Boyd motioned in an animated fashion with his hands.

"No Boyd..." Adair tried to say.

"You thick-headed lumix. Adair is all moony for her."

Boyd stopped. One could almost see the cogs turning. More coffee spilt as he laughed and slammed the coffee down on the table. "Oh My GOD! Adair - what are you - 15?"

Adair frowned and turned back to the balcony. Behind his back Delilah shot Boyd dirty looks to try to shut up his laughing. "Don't worry Adair. I can help here too." she said quietly.

-- == == --

"Adair, you have a MESH from Delilah. Would you like to take it, or should I tell her you are unavailable?" Elisha asked in quiet even tones.

Adair was hunched over the desk in his room, putting the final touches on his Ethics and Morality paper. He glanced at the clock - Eleven-Forty-Six. He should have gone to bed already... but lost track of time. "Sure. Put her on"

A small window opened, and Adair dragged it down from the wall to his desk-top. Delilah was there, but it was difficult to see where she was. "Hey you. Looking good. Can we talk?" Faint music could be heard, and from time to time Delilah was jostled.

"I thought we are talking. Where are you?"

"No - in person. Meet me in the caf." Delilah glanced away from the screen, and not giving Adair a chance to answer she smiled. "See you soon." and cut connection.

Adair was about to protest when the connection ended. "Would you like me to re-establish connection, Cadet Fox?"

Adair reached up to rub his eyes. "No. That will be alright. Save my work please."

The open folders and papers folded neatly away and disappeared into the aethers. As Adair stood up, the blank wall returned to pictures of the scenic river, slowly panning down in the darkness. The wall was set to mimic the light levels outside, and the moon reflected off the water and the trees swayed in the wind. Adair paused to watch the scenery for a moment, then pulling his footwear on, he headed out across the quad.

-- == == --

Outside was another late fall shower, and while the distance between the dorms and the rec hall was small, Adair was soaked by the time he got to the large public building. The entire time he was wondering what Delilah could want to talk about - and why it couldn't wait until tomorrow, and why they couldn't use the MESH. But the, after everything which had happened recently - Adair was growing more and more suspicious of the MESH and of Elisha in particular. If it wasn't the teachers, then it was like the MESH itself or the AI's connected to it were actively cheating. And the professors either weren't willing to accept it, or were ignoring the facts.

The cafe was eerily empty at the late hour. The holo pits sat empty and dark, and all of the food concessions were closed. Adair didn't see Delilah around. It was strange being in the large dark rec hall without anyone else in it. He headed up the staircase to the second-floor - heading to their usual perch at the balcony. He could watch out over the room, and besides after the last couple weeks this table felt like a second home to him.

There was a faint smell in the air - something vaguely fruity. Like passion fruit and coconut. Reaching up to wipe a wet bang plastered to his face, he looked over the edge, and nearly fell when a soft voice spoke behind him.

"Excuse me, have you seen Delilah Telford around? Oh... it's you."

Adair spun around to be face to face with the mystery woman from the simulation. Her hair was shorter - of course, and she was dressed in the grey and blue uniform of the academy. She carried a mug of steaming tea in her hands, and her wide deep brown eyes sparkled in the dim light.

Adair just stood there - dripping.

"I guess I was not meant to meet Delilah here." She spoke, a soft shy smile on her lips, "Hi."

"Hi." Adair stammered.

"You didn't have to get drenched. I would have still recognized you."

Adair reached up, pushing his wet hair back. "It's - raining out."

"I know. I took the underground tunnels."

"Oh. I never heard of them." Adair blushed. A slight awkward silence fell as Adair reached for something to say. So far she was leading the entire conversation.

"I'm Adair. Adair Fox."

"I know." She gave a little laugh. "I think everyone knows you. You are the one who keeps blowing everything up. She still smiled that mysterious shy smile. She looked down and then back up. "You know, some warm hot tea would help keep the chills away. I find the weather here so damp and cold." When she spoke, there was a slight french accent to her speech, and she spoke with the perfect english of a diplomat or aristocrat.

"Why are you here?" Adair asked, trying to understand the situation.

She thought for a moment, moving to set the tea down and sitting in one of the chairs opposite Adair. "Well, after the simulation, Trevor was upset. Everyone was there when the computer told him where to stop you. Even though he won, he felt it tarnished it by cheating. He actually blamed you and your MESH hacker friend."

She sat down, reaching up to brush back hair that wasn't there. Obviously before she joined the academy she was used to having long hair, as she did in the simulation. "I wanted to talk to Delilah, and it was not hard to look her up on the MESH. We talked about the simulation," She paused, her brown eyes looking into Adair as she leaves out more of their conversation, "And how strange things have been. Then she suggested we meet here."

"That doesn't make sense. I mean nothing has really made sense this year, but why would she want to meet at midnight." His shyness was being ablated, and Adair was finding it easy to talk. To trust this woman.

"I think talking about the school was not what Miss Telford had in mind." She smiled realizing the game that Delilah was up to.

"You didn't talk about me, with Delilah, did you?" Adair was slowly clueing in too.

She just smiled in response. "You can drink that tea. I can get another. You need it more than I do." She reached for the steaming cup and slide it towards Adair.

Adair reached forward, and for a brief moment, his fingertips touched hers. She withdrew her long slender fingers, and he brought the cup up to his lips. He was about to point out that he still didn't know her name.

"You can call me Al. It is short for Alphosine. It's not a very common name."
The tea wasn't the standard earl-grey that the dispensary served. It was the source of those smells, and had an exotic mixture of island fruits and coconut. Warm and soothing.

"Neither is Adair. I think my folks were going through that 'strange baby name' phase where everyone was trying to outdo each other in how exotic names could be." Adair set the tea down, and climbed up to perch on a seat opposite Alphosine. "You said warm - are you from the caribbean?"

She smiled and shook her head. "Wrong side of the planet. You would not know my island. It is a tiny volcanic island in the South Pacific."

"And you ended up here. I bet you have some story to tell. I'm from Canada - it's a large country north of the US"

She smiled. "I'm familiar with it. I originally joined the United World in the diplomatic circles. It is an accident that I ended up enrolling here. My father was furious." She shifted in her chair. "I like the freedom and all of the interesting people. And with the United World Space Force - I'll meet people literally not from Earth."

The two talked into the night.

-- == == --

Boyd leant over and nudged Adair. It was the second time that his eyes had closed and his head had started to droop. The action was unnoticed by the rest of the class – for now. They were gathered in the main lecture hall, and the dim lights made it easy to drift off.

"What's with you?" Boyd whispered. "Were you up late or something?"

On the other side of him, Delilah smiled a knowing smile.

"No. Just didn't sleep last night." Adair made an excuse.

The teacher was explaining the next simulation. The group was being divided and it was a competition. The cadets were being divided into teams of twenty who would be veying in a number of competitions. As the team leaders were handed out, Adair leant forward in his seat only to be passed up time and time again. Cadets with lesser knowledge, and with lesser experience were being chosen and Adair was not being given a second consideration.

When it was time to start building the teams, Adair was disillusioned. The trio knew that the powers-that-be were purposely not giving him any command authority. Once all of the leaders for the exercise had been chosen, the group of team leaders came down to the center of the large hall to started calling out names. Christina Griggs was one of the first ones up, and looking up at the Adair-Boyd-Delilah trio, she called out "Delilah Telford"

Delilah reached to give Adair's shoulder a squeeze as she wandered down to join her group.

Boyd was picked moments later. The selection continued down the line of team leaders until it got to McDuff.

"Adair Fox." He said. His group was broken up. With a sigh, Adair walked down to the empty section in the hall. As the other captains went forward, Duff came close to Adair. His face was one of frustration.

"Hey Fox. I know that everyone said I cheated to win the last event." Adair looked up cautiously, not wanting to start a confrontation.

"I know you had nothing to do with it. And I think it's rotten that someone is stooping to that level. But if they want to play like that – then fine. If they don't want to play fair, then let's not play fair." His eyes bristled with rebellion. Perhaps too much so.

"I want you to not feel like I'm holding you back. I know that others like Griggs and Tomat – they think that you're just a devious little trickster. Well I want you to pull every trick in the book. If they want to throw the rules away – so can we."

Adair thought about that, and then nodded.

"Well... how do we start?"

Adair knew that his friends had already been chosen, and while they were talking out of the corner of his eye he saw Alphosine get picked.

"Well... we need diversification. See how Tomak is getting all of the power-houses. Boyd, people like that. It's great for the physical challenges, but it leaves him vulnerable for more creative ones."

McDuff nodded, and when his turn came up, he looked to Adair for advice on who to pick. The two of them started building a team. One by one, they picked a diverse group – choosing cadets which may have otherwise been initially passed over. They concentrated too on personality, picking people who would allow them to form a tight-knit team.

After the team selection, Professor Sparling put up the outline of the first team challenge. It would be a confidence course, otherwise known as an old-fashioned obstacle course. The group was to be graded as a total combined sum of the entire team.

Adair leaned over to whisper to McDuff, who raised his hands. "What are the rules, tho.. what are the limits?"

Professor Sparling looked over, his gaze settling on Adair – not on McDuff. "You are to run the course – not skipping any of the stations. And Adair – for all of our sakes, we have removed the explosives from the sim. Please do not try to blow up the course."

The collected cadets chuckled. "You have two hours to prepare. We will then start running the course – four teams at a time. The schedule will be posted outside the Immersion Chamber."

The cadets left the lecture hall in small groups, with the team leaders giving directions on where the group were to meet up to use their two hour prep-time.

Team McDuff (as they started calling themselves) retired to one of the corners of the rec hall, pulling several tables over. They went over some of the strategy, and looked at the specific rules Professor Sparling had provided as well as the specific obstacles they were about to face. At times one of the cadets would question the nuances that Adair was coming up with – to which McDuff would answer – "Anything not restricted is allowed."

-- == == --

The simulation formed in someplace which could have been in northern England – or really any temperate area. There were open stretches and at times the confidence course wound it's way in and out of a nearby small forest. The trees were a mixture of deciduous and coniferous, and the ground actually had little in the way of underbrush or shrubs. A large scoreboard had the time readouts for the teams. Several of the earlier teams had D.N.F. instead of times, while the times varied widely from 15:43 (the best time posted so far) to 59:45.

The four teams milled in the staging field. Around them the voice of Professor Sparling boomed, announcing the first team. Adair lined up along the side with the rest of his team, to watch the other teams compete.

The first team lined up, and sent their people through the course one after another. There were different stations which caused the occasional bottleneck - and because of the varying fitness levels, the more athletic would charge through leaving those with lesser abilities behind. Adair studied the course carefully, and then went over to McDuff. "We need to go last."

McDuff stalked off to talk to the rival captain and Adair noticed that Boyd's team was going next. Boyd caught his eye and gave a friendly wave. He then pointed at the clock and made a strange unknown gesture. Presumably he was challenging Adair to a competition. At a purely physical challenge - Boyd had the clear advantage.

Some loud shouts brought attention to the nearby team where McDuff was being restrained - it looked like his talk with the other captain nearly ended in blows. He was pulled away, and finally stalked back to his team in mock anger. Coming by Adair, he gave him a wink. Over at the other team they were rallying and cheering and heading to the starting line.

Adair looked up at the time, as Boyd and his team posted an admirable 13:51 - shaving over a minute off the previous best time. He know Boyd would be proud of their team's achievement, and he felt good for his friend. As the team before theirs queued up, McDuff pulled his team into a huddle.

"Okay Adair - we're up. So, what is the plan."

Adair smirked, and started talking quickly. He had about fifteen minutes to relay what they were about to do.

-- == == --

Agiprom Prime Centri sat in his room with his twin pairs of arms crossed over his chest. With his implants, he did not require the crude technology which the humans utilized to be able to monitor the Immersion simulation currently underway. Using his diplomatic credentials, he joined the large group of observers. Already having reviewed all of the cadet identified as Adair Fox, he had singled this human out for his unconventional thinking. Ignoring the incessant babbling of Under-Secretary-General Wakelin, he felt a tickle at the edge of his consciousness. Unable to focus on it, he ignored it and watched the events unfold.

-- == == --

If there was a human equivalent, Kh't L'nkt would be frustrated with a dabble of wrath spiced with revenge. Scanning the simulation it saw that now this Adair human had drawn the attention of the Mara. The D'rak N'li had to tread carefully, as Mara was much more sensitive to its presence in the primitive human simulation. Careful to mask its influence Kh't L'nkt set forth to sabotage the simulation.

-- == == --

McDuff lead his team to the starting line. Unlike other teams who would start in a single file, or a loose collected mob, they had formed up into a tight group of 4 lines of 5 cadets. McDuff and Adair were in the second rank - the first rank consisted of the burly team members. McDuff and Adair were surrounded by the more lithe and quick members, and the rest of the team formed the rank and file behind them. A whistle sounded the start of the run. Unlike the rest of the teams, the entire group started off. The first line broke away from the pack and sprinted towards the first obstacle - a vertical twelve foot wooden rough-hewn wall.

Reaching the wall ahead of the group, the four quickly formed up. Three of them dropped to their hands and knees, with Alonso, a burley spaniard climbing up onto the back of Ned. The remaining cadet helped braced Alonso, and knelt down to provide his shoulders. The effect was to make a human staircase going up the wall.

Closing on the first obstacle, the 4 lines interlaced and formed one continuous row, McDuff in the lead. Without breaking stride the entire group climbed the staircase and vaulted over the wall. Landing first on the other side, McDuff and Adair stepped to the side to help the cadets land and continue forward. The entire group crossed in record time, with the remaining four clambering over the walls, joining the ranks at the tail of the group as the line continued on.

Cadets watched in stunned amazement - a couple of the initial protests of 'cheating' were quieted as McDuff's group approached the next obstacle. Low-strung barbed wire forced cadets to crawl, greatly slowing the pace.

Now with smaller agile people in the lead, they scurried under the first strands, and carefully avoiding the barbs they stood up, in the process lifting several of the barbed wire strands up. Two more cadets scurried forward, repeating the action.

The main group approached the four lines merging into two. The lead members scurried forward, repeating the actions until the entire obstacle was neutralized. The rest of the group passed the barbed wire by ducking and continuing through unabated. As the group passed, the first cadets released their wires and joined the tail end - the group reforming into four lines as they continued.

Next was a 'balance beam' type set of wooden logs suspended up into the trees. Forming a single file, and linking arms, the group turned into one gestalt form - each person helping to form a 'safety line' for the entire group to work across the log.

-- == == --

Kh't L'nkt resisted the urge to scream out in frustration. It was like the human fiction titled 'Leningrad versus the ants'. But Kh't L'nkt had more at his disposal than Leningrad - he could control the laws of reality itself. Metaphysically reaching into the code-base, his fingers delicately touched configurations that were supposedly untouchable, and started giving a little twist. Oxygen content was lower from 20% to 5%. The gravitational setting was increased from 1.0G to 2.2G.

-- == == --

Adair had suspected something like this would occur. It was clearly getting difficult to breathe, and suddenly he was carrying double his weight across his shoulders. In the fields of observation most of the cadets sat or laid down, gulping for air. A raspy cry gave out - one of the last cadets stumbled off the beam, falling eighteen inches to the ground. Claire Mc Ferguson had broken her leg from the fall, even though it was only a short distance.

"Link up - you can do it." Adair croaked - his chest felt like it had an anvil on it. He gasped for air that wasn't there.

Linking their arms like they did previously, the group persevered. Pushing onward they approached a muddy pit where the objective was to swing across ropes. The increased gravity caused the wooden cross-members to bow down from the weight of the ropes, and the mud was glassy smooth.

"Same plan as before - just be very careful lowering the stones in place."

Adair commented.

"Keep it up - you can see how they are doing everything they can to stop us." McDuff continued rallying the troops. Him and Adair went to the front, and helped lower some of the larger cadets into the mire. The cadets in the mire slowly waded across, up to their shoulders in the muck, and reached to link arms to shoulders - forming a bridge.

The rest of the cadets formed a single file, again linking hands to shoulders to help support each other. Claire had a steely look in her eyes as she resisted the offer to be carried across and limped on the broken ankle.

The challenges weren't over. As the group started to cross, bubbles appeared in the mud. Adair noticed the look on the cadets they were all using as a bridge. The mud was heating up.

"Double time! We need to get across now!"

Doubling their pace, the entire group crossed the muddy pool - the entire group forming a chain to help pull their stepping stones out of the mud. By this time, the pool was bubbling like crazy, and the last two cadets - Alonso and Ned - were badly burnt. They gasped for air, but continued onward.

The group formed up, cadets on either side supporting Alonso, Ned, Claire and every other cadet who was struggling after the ordeal. Crossing the line, Adair glanced up, noticing the timer as he fell to the ground - blissfully passing out before he landed with a bone-snapping crunch. The team had crossed in under ten minutes.

-- == == --

The Immersion Chamber was flooded with staff. Interposed between the people was Elisha's hologram. Medical staff had portable respirators on many of the cadets and technicians had wall panels out attempting to override the computer.

"This one is crashing - get a respirator over here."

"Can't we just pull them out!"

"I'm sorry, I'm unable to comply with that command."

Professor Sparling stood in the middle of the storm - the eye of the hurricane of activity. "Has anyone managed to trace how we lost control of the system."

"MESH technicians are working on it, Sir."

-- == == --

Agiprom Prime Centri was able to monitor the situation as he crossed from the suite towards the exit. Another part of his mind was dedicated to sharing this particular feed with the other Agiprom Primes across the planet. Another part was busy preparing the Mara Drop-craft.

His mine worked faster than any human could perceive it - moving around the clumsy tools which the humans were using to trying to undo the damage. This was far too elegant - too sophisticated to have a human source.

Doors slide open and closed behind him as he crossed the platform to the unfolding ramp being extended from his Drop-craft. Systems started to power up.

"Ah. Yes. Here is the source of the blocks." Centri was able to release all of the restraints on the system settings. Control instantly reverted back to the humans - the locks also having the unfortunate side effect of deleting their footprint. Of course Mara technicians could coax the subtle traces to determine the source of the sabotage.

Centri was still focusing primarily on the MESH, and did not notice the indicator on his display until it was too late.

Ultra-high energy scalar mesons crashed into the unshielded hull of the Mara Drop-craft as it was powering up. Atoms were ripped apart, and the beam was directed at the drive-core producing a momentary fusion cascade.

The resulting explosion reduced most of the craft to atomic particles, and left a two hundred foot crater in the side of the Spanish Visitation Diplomatic site.

The electromagnetically masked asked D'rak N'li craft folded back into the hyper-dimensions not accessible by human-kind.

-- == == --

Breathable air suddenly flowed into Adair's lungs. He coughed and sat up, his muscles cramping from where they were clenching. Apparently the Immersion was also adversely affecting the real bodies of the students. The Immersion Chamber was in chaos.

This couldn't be the work of the staff. His previous theories of the staff made no sense. Especially for such an overt obvious assault against the student body. He managed to stand up, his legs quivering, and made his way over to the Immersion chair for Boyd. There was a respirator over his head, and a portable breathing pack beside him. He leaned on the table, reading the display.

"Your friend is going to be okay. He's just suffering from mild hypoxia."

Adair looked up in appreciation at the medical technician who went over to deal with other patents.

There was a sudden commotion by the door, and Delilah writhed past the guards, running into the room and over to wrap her arms around Adair.

"Are you alright? We were watching on the monitors... everyone was. What were you thinking?"

Adair let himself collapse into Delilah's arms, enjoying the momentary support.

"Why didn't you stop? Why did you keep going?"

"We can't let them win." Adair smiled, and looked across to where McDuff was sitting up on his bench. He looked back and smiled broadly at Adair.

Coughing behind them muffled by the respirator masked announced that Boyd was waking up. Gently releasing Adair, Delilah knelt down, running her hand through Boyd's short curly black hair.

"What did I miss?" Boyd joked weakly.

"You always were trouble to wake up after an Immersion sim - you big lummox" Delilah laid down and nuzzled Boyd.

6

Negotiations with Humanity is complicated at the best of times, and a minefield of conflicting interests nearly all of the time.

In theory, the United World represented Earth, however the United World Space Force was only one of three major powers with a substantial space navy, without including the twenty civilian corporations which also had spaceflight capability. Civilian vessels were prevented from being armed, however they outnumbered the military ships roughly 3 to 1.

Humanity had spread to numerous orbital and ground bases throughout the solar system - from the floating Ishtar Venusian Research Base floating in the upper cloud deck of Venus to the ill-fated Lassell Outpost on the frozen moon of Triton. Two bases; Armstrong Base on the Moon and Cyril Base on Mars had sought independence and were recognized as sovereign nations. Other stations, such as Gateway and Voyager were operated by the United World Space Force and were open to all residents of the Earth.

The Hegemony had vastly different rules when dealing with Non-Hegemony civilizations. All official contact and negotiations were handled by a specially genetically altered contact race. Contact between other Hegemony member races was strictly forbidden.

> *The contact races were under strict guidelines about their interactions with Non-Hegemony civilizations. They were forbidden to interfere with their development - technologically or socially. There was a complicated set of requirements before a civilization could apply for membership inside the Hegemony. Unfortunately many of these requirements were not shared with civilizations as they would interfere with the development - thus races had to 'stumble' through a set of requirements unknown to them.*
>
> *There were also not the same protections offered to Non-Hegemony civilizations, which would allow at times more opportunistic Hegemonic races to exploit the younger races for their own gains. This would need to occur behind the watchful eye of the contact race.*
>
> *An even less broached subject are the fact of races who after meeting the requirements do not wish to join the Hegemony. It takes a truly powerful or unique race to stand up to the combined force and influence of the Hegemony.*
>
> ``Becoming One''
> *Secretary-General Shelley Dione (ret.), UWSF - 2031*

Medical staff had checked and cleared all of the students. There was some minor muscle pulls, but no lasting damage. There was heightened tension in the air that was almost tangible. Armed UWSF marines were present at major public nexus, and there were four Mara Agriprom Primes who were on the campus grounds. World-wide, most of the Mara had been recalled, leaving world government scrambling for explanation. The academy was on an information lock-down but tried to continue classes as normal as possible.

Adair, Boyd and Delilah were in the Rec center, perched at the balcony overlooking the room below. Technicians had recently cleared the Immersion Chamber for use again, but students were anxious. There were murmurs of terrorists, sabotage and conspiracy theories.

Boyd was the first to notice the approaching group of women, and straightened up, putting on his charming smile. "Ladies, welcome! Boyd is here to make your afternoon better"

Delilah rolled her eyes and looked over, nudging Adair who was lost in thought staring over the edge.

The cluster of women shifted, and Alphosine stepped to the forefront. "Hi

Adair." A couple of her friends stifled juvenile little giggles. "I am glad you are alright. I heard about what happened in the simulation."

Boyd glanced over curious as he's completely ignored. "I'm alright too, you know... hey?"

Delilah had stood up and taken Boyd's arm. "Boyd, why don't we go down and get something to eat." She smiled at the women who were also giving Alphosine their farewells. "He's so clueless sometimes." referring to Boyd. The women giggled in their agreement with Delilah.

Adair watched everyone leave and then over to Alphosine as she came closer.

"Um... everyone didn't have to leave."

"I am still shy." Alphosine admitted, "When I told my friends they insisted I come and talk to you."

"I'm glad you did. I liked our talk we had the other night."

Alphosine came closer, reaching up to Adair's arm. "Are you sure you are well? I heard that a couple of your classmates had torn muscles. I thought that was not able to happen when we were in the chamber."

Adair liked her touch. "The body kept reacting, even through the neuro-suppressants. All the safeguards were over-ridden. They assure us that we were still safe - but I wonder what if someone died in there. Would their body just think that it died, and shut down."

There was a commotion below, and Adair and Alphosine glanced over the edge. One of the Agriprom Prime had entered the building and was drawing attention. Cadets tried to get a close look at the alien without getting close enough to draw attention to themselves. Most people had never seen one live before - until now the aliens were something you saw on the MESH screen talking to high-ranking diplomats.

"I wonder why they are here?" Adair wondered aloud. He felt the gentle pressure of Alphosine on his arm, and shifted so she could get a better look. Adair found he couldn't give much attention to the Mara. Even though Adair was shorter than average, he still had several inches on Alphosine. He looked at the back of her head and inhaled, enjoying her faintly tropical scent. He found her presence utterly distracting.

"I heard from my father that they had pulled out worldwide. The majority of the V&M offices have closed. There was an incident and the UWSF is covering it up. The Americans and Chinese are furious, however the Secretary-General is claiming this is an internal issue. There is also pressure from the Russians and Indians and some groups are looking at bringing a proposal to the permanent members to have an independant group review the UWSF."

He turned, looking into her light brown eyes. He's amazed at how politically knowledgeable she was, and it was very easy to just be lost in her eyes.

"What did I say?" Alphosine blushed as she caught Adair just staring.

"Nothing - I'm sorry. I was…" he trailed off - not really having an excuse.

She giggled and smiled. "It is okay. You are so charming."

The air between them shifted - an almost tangible change. The pair looked over to where the Mara had climbed the stairs with it's long spindly legs, and had unfolded both pairs of arms in a gesture of greeting.

"Greetings be to you, Cadet Fox Adair and Ol'hea Cadet Brial-Fuluhea Alphosine. My name is Agriprom Intirum Ciltra of the Hegemony Visitation and Monitoring Envoy."

Alphosine mimicked the gesture with quite a level of grace and timing; Adair did the best he could as well. She then gave Adair a soft nudge.

"Umm.. Greetings be to you, Agriprom Prime Sil-tra."

"That's Ciltra." Alphosine whispered in his ear. "softer c sound - like in cell"

"Please excuse my interruption. I seek to be granted opportunity to exchange conversation with Cadet Fox Adair." Ciltra closed his arms, standing fully erect causing Adair and Alphosine to crane their head to look up at the alien.

The pair looked at each other.

"I will see you later Adair." Alphosine gave her winning smile, and then ducked away. Around them cadets and faculty were curious.

"Sure." he watched her leave and then brought his attention back to the alien. "I think there are some small club rooms. We could use one of those."

Adair turned and lead the Mara towards where some clubs rooms were available. Normally they were to be signed out, but he suspected this was pretty far from normal. Besides half the people watching were faculty.

The lights in the small room flared to life as Adair opened the door. Ciltra walked in, ducking his head and shoulders to move through the small door frame, and walked to one side of the table. "A seat may be used if it pleases you."

Adair moved to the other side of the table, but choose to remain standing.

"There have been relations between the Mara and humanity for a decade of your time." When he talked Ciltra gestured occasionally with his smaller lower pair of hands. Adair kept looking up at the vaguely insect-like face.

"That is true, although we have not had contact with the other races of the Hegemony."

"That is the way things are done. Humanity is not yet ready - humanity is impulsive, rash, and reactive. You are a young race who seeks to run before you can walk." Ciltra's fingers interlace in a complex manner.

"You did not ask me here to discuss our shortfalls." Adair didn't back down from the direct contact with the alien. "You want to discuss what happened in the Immersion Chamber."

Ciltra's fingers unlaced. "Direct. Very much like a human." Inwardly he was still assessing Adair. "There was a computer malfunction with the training exercise yesterday."

Adair shook his head. "We both know that is not true. The Immersion Chamber - heck the MESH itself are alien technology which was adopted by us. And a glitch would have shown up as a glitch - not an alteration purposely targeted. The teachers should have maintained control, but control was locked away. And the Mara leaving Earth - and yet there are now Intirum - a rank never before on Earth - here. Not only was this not an accident - this was done by some faction within the Hegemony, and you don't know who." His voice didn't change inflection as Adair finally had an outlet.

Ciltra was silent. He looked up at the omnipresent monitoring devices - this place was not secure. Unfolding it's arms in a formal greeting. "I have learned what I have come to learn. Please be well, Cadel Fox Adair."

Adair stepped between Ciltra and the door. "That's your way, isn't it? The Mara don't give any help - you just are here to placate. In a decade, all of the advancements humanity didn't 'earn' - and you were opposed to every step of the way. MESH - the FT Hop - all of the advances we gained through other channels."

Ciltra glowered down at Adair. "Humanity is not ready for any of these things. There are ways things are done. Humanity has not yet earned it's place in the Hegemony and lunges blindly ahead into a future it is not prepared for." Ciltra stops before Adair.

"I think humanity has some surprises in store for you and the Hegemony." Adair stepped aside.

-- == == --

Adair found Alphosine sitting with her friends on a table outside the rec center. He recognized her friends from some of the other classes and sims. He had just stood one on one with one of the Mara - so he should be able to take on a few women.

The conversation stopped as he approached. Alphosine looked up with an expectant smile.

"Hi Alphosine. Hi." he greeted the rest of the table too. There were a soft reply of greetings.

"I'm sorry about that, I'd like to continue talking, if now is a good time?"

Alphosine stands up. "Sure. You have met my friends ..."

Acting uncommon for Elisha, she interrupts the conversation. Her voice is small, coming from Adair's wrist. "Cadet Adair Fox. You are to report to Professor Sparling's office. Please acknowledge receipt of this summons."

Everyone looked down at his wrist, and then back up to Adair. Adair didn't both lifting his wrist, letting out a long breath.

"I'm sorry - it looks like fate isn't done with me yet. Umm later?" He gives Alphosine an apologetic look.

"Do not worry. I can at least walk you there." She stands up, picking up her tea. "I will see you later" she bid her friends farewell, and formed up with Adair.

"What did Ciltra want?" She pauses to discard her container as they crossed before the building heading towards administration.

"I'm not sure. He talked around the issues - he seemed to want to more talk about Humanity and the Hegemony."

"He is a diplomat. I do not think he would be cleared to say more."

"I'm not sure. Even his title - I've never heard of an Intirum before. I think something is up - something big. He kept talking about humanity and how we were not ready."

The pair passed into the administration building. The marble lined halls were mostly empty, except for the omnipresence of Elisha.

"There are always rumours of what the governments are really up to. Some say we have already started to explore nearby star systems. Maybe humans are crossing into someone else's territory - breaking some space-laws that we are not aware of."

"But they don't share those laws with us. The Mara have been coddling and holding back from us since day one. They were furious when we got the FT-Hop Drive, and they just stood back and didn't help during the Neptune tragedy."
"Just be careful Adair. I feel this is larger than you and I - larger than the school."

Adair gives a roguish smile, and winks at Alphosine. "Don't worry about me. I'm always careful." He opens the door and steps into Professor Sparling's office.

-- == == --

The office reflected Professor Sparling. There were a couple paintings - not computer imagery but real oil and canvas paintings depicting snowy fields and trees. The room had a small functional grey desk, and a glass fronted cabinet which had various medals and awards, along with a couple personal effects. There was an old leather ball glove, some photos (in a digital frame) showing various stages of a younger Sparling and people from his past, and a small armillary sphere.

The professor was behind his desk and didn't get up as Adair entered. His close-cropped red hair was bright with the light streaming in through the window, and when he looked up, his brown eyes looked weary.

"I understand you had a recent visitor."

Adair assumed an attention stance. It wasn't a question, so he merely stood there.

"Fox - I've had a long day as you can imagine. I fight very hard for to protect my cadets - and that includes you." He waved his hand over the holo-displays, and the MESH connection was cut.

Adair stayed at attention. He then pointedly looked down at the desk. Even turned off, Elisha was constantly listening. The professor looked down, and then back up at Adair. "Let's go for a walk."

He stood up, taking his dress jacket off from behind the chair, and lead Adair out of the office. They continued walking through the administration building in silence, out across the quad, and down towards where some new buildings were under construction. The work had paused as the builders had uncovered some Roman artifacts. The professor unlocked a gate and the two walked down a hastily made staircase down to where century old broken fallen columns had been unearthed.

"I think it's safe to say we are away from influences here."

Adair looked around. It was virtually impossible to be completely out of range - unless one truly went out into the wilderness.

"The Mara are at the school investigating the incident. But it's bigger than that."

The professor nodded. "Go on."

"I think it was one of the other aliens who did the attack. And they would have had the means. Our systems are secure - but it's all built on the fundamental framework the aliens sold to us. It's easy to imagine that there are backdoors."

"That sounds reasonable. Why you, Adair?"

"I don't know. It was strange - the Mara spoke about humanity and our place - but I'm just a Cadet here." He looked up at the professor. "I used to think that you were intentionally singling me out."

The professor pursed his lips, examining the centuries old column without touching it. He turned and looked at Adair. "I have been - for some time. We have some good cadets in the school Adair. But you are a good commander. You think outside the box and yet you still have ethics which you will not betray. You can be defiant, but that is your youth. And you inspire greatness in others."

Adair didn't say anything, listening to the assessment. "There are others - Trevor, Christina… "

"Sure - I didn't say you were the only great commander. But I suspect that they are also facing some of the same adversary. You graduates will be our next era of great captains. Just when humans are leaving Earth. Perhaps that is why you are targetted."

"But the UWSF has captains. There are ships already out there."

"Of course. But those captains come from our old thinking. The world they grew up in was small - finite. You will be the first era in this new age."

"But the Mara - Ciltra. He didn't really say anything. Just a lot of double-talk."

"If you look back over the last decade, you will see that has been the same for most of the diplomatic exchanges. Most of the true technological advances came from private dealings behind the back of the Mara. And most of the diplomatic overtures has been damage control. There is much talk of 'Humanity is not ready' and 'We do not understand the rules of the Hegemony' and yet no steps to teach us."

"Maybe that's why we have been given this technology. Someone wants us to fail - wants us to break some rules we're not aware of to doom Humanity." Adair thought for a moment. "It's just like the sims where we aren't even aware of the twists but we still need to achieve the objectives."

The professor thought about this and nodded. "That may be. But you cannot let us down - Adair. If Ciltra - or any of the other Mara talk to you, or if you just wish to talk let me know. I will always have time for you."

7

When mankind first visited the moon, it was for scientific reasons. Mankind stopped due to budgetary cut-backs, and when mankind first returned to the moon, it was for these same budgetary reasons. With the boon in space-born construction, it was initially cheaper to mine and refine raw materials from the moon regolith.

Spurred on by private industry, the first bases were automated or teleoperated, and would collect and process materials to be stockpiled. Later, Webb Resources landed the first electromagnetic railgun allowing processed materials to be shot into a 'catcher' in Low-Lunar Orbit. This greatly sped up and provided a constant plentiful supply of materials for near earth constructions.

Armstrong Base had been build and settled long before the public arrival of the Hegemony. Armstrong Base was originally named Constellation Outpost and was first established by the National Aeronautics and Space Administration, a now defunct agency of the United States of America in 2012. The original structures were not designed for permanent habitation, but temporary stays while manned missions were visiting the surface. The base had robotic in-situ processing which would continue to mine and produce raw material and expand the base in-between manned visitations. Constellation Outpost was established in Shackleton Crater, and permitted monitoring, oversight and a manned presence on the moon.

The base was nearly abandoned in 2015 following the rise in global tension, then as the attention once again returned to the skies Eapo reactors and new advancements in spaceflight coupled with an extensive growing private fleet of spacecraft rapidly expanded Constellation Outpost. With ample in-situ resources, the base expanded rapidly and quickly became the central hub for Lunar activity. Several major companies were based in Armstrong and the base had even opened several remote bases.

By 2016 the base had seen 500% - 800% growth, and the base had expanded from being a United States government facility to a multi-national outpost which had a number of non-scientific / military inhabitants. In 2017, Armstrong Base was the site for the first human born off of Earth (aptly named Luna Tsiu) and the population had started including researches and corporate employees who were on indefinite contract - not set to return to Earth.

In March of 2018, citizens at Constellation Outpost filed with both the United States of America; NASA had been disbanded in 2017, government space operations were now handled by the Air Force Space Program Command (AFSPC); and with the United Nations for independent sovereign recognition. The base was still heavily dependant on the Earth for supplies, however it would exchange these for locally produced raw materials for power and construction, low-gravity environments for specialty assembly and specialty research which could not be conducted on Earth.

August 18, 2019 formed the birth of Armstrong Base - the first extra-Earth independant territory. While it only had an initial population of 875 citizens, it quickly grew over the next decade to have over 1,800 permanent residence.

excerpt "Armstrong Base - History"
MESH wikia, 2023

With the Immersion Chambers offline for a detailed teardown and inspection, the curriculum was vastly upset. Without the use of the chamber, the teachers had to resort to alternate mechanisms for relaying their class content. Practical simulations were cancelled altogether and the cadets found themselves with more time.

Adair laid on his bed listening to New Horizenz - an electro-synth band while the walls flickered between pictures of his home-town. Snow covered fields and tall broad-limbed trees with their boughs heavy with snow covered rustic looking houses along the streets. Decorative festive lights and sparkly tinsel was twisted into generic holiday shapes and cast multicolour traces on the branches and streets. Outside the window - it was still T-shirt weather in the south of Spain.

The door chimed, and slide open. Adair looked up to see Delilah entering.

"Heyas Fox." Delilah wasn't wearing her cadet uniform - but instead was a functional however slightly plain rust-coloured blouse and beige slacks. Her UWSF badge hung at her waist.

"Hey. You're dressed up - where are you off to?" Adair still wore his cadet uniform - mostly out of habit. Most of his civilian clothing was far too warm for this climate, and he never bothered to get replacements due to the grueling training schedule.

"I thought we could take a little trip. What with Boyd being gone, and having a 4 day weekend - you could talk Professor Sparling into getting us a pass."

"Why me?" Adair's tone wasn't too strong. It would be nice to get away - he just didn't really have any ideas of where to go.

"Because you're his favourite - duh! Just get us passes, and meet me at the landing pad."

Adair paused, and as Delilah turned to go. "What about Alphosine?"

There was a slight pause. Jealous? Adair couldn't tell. "Sure... you can bring her along too. But hurry - time is ticking." She didn't look back as she left.

Adair pushed himself up and decided instead of MESHing Alphosine, but instead to ask her in person.

"Elisha, please locate Alphosine."

"Alphosine is in the Cadet Rec Hall, First Floor. Would you like me to contact her via MESH?"

"No thank you. I'll go myself."

Adair headed to the door - the walls flickering off and the music silencing as soon as he left the room.

-- == == --

The Rec Hall wasn't as busy as it should have been - many of the cadets having already left taking advantage of the long weekend. Only about half of those present were in the typical grey and cobalt blue uniforms; the rest of the cadets wore many bright colours and flowing fabrics of modern fashion styles. The conversations were animated and positive. There was an feeling of joy and carefree happiness in the air.

Alphosine was sitting with two of her regular close friends. The group was talking in quick-animated French interspersed with laughter. The group smiled and made room when Adair came close. Her friends were definitely from a different social and economic background - however they have grown to accept Adair.

"Hi Alphosine. Hi Sophie and Carmeline." The girls were all dressed in the very latest haute-couture. Tasteful gems and pearls danced inside their outfits. One of their blouses would probably be worth more than Adair's entire wardrobe.

"Hi Adair, sit with us." Sophie shifted over at Alphosine's invitation so that Adair could sit between them. All of the eyes were on him as he joined.

"We were talking about how to take advantage of this long weekend." Alphosine started.

"You mean we had decided that we needed a girl's shopping trip to Paris, Al!" Carmeline chimed in. Alphosine turned and gave her a look. She then turned back to Adair.

"I was going to talk to you at supper. I wanted to see if you were okay if I went away." Her tone was careful trying to gauge Adair's reaction. It was clearly implied that this meant just the girls going away - not an invitation to Adair.

"Of course I'd be okay. I was coming to ask you if you wanted to come away with Delilah and myself. But if you have plans, that's okay." Adair's voice was sincere.

Sophie and Carmeline looked at Alphosine - not wanting to pressure her but to say 'you're going to choose him over coming away shopping with us?' Alphosine reached to take Adair's hand - her fingers short and slender as they wrapped around his hand.

"Are you sure, Adair? It would be fun to come away - where are you going?"

Adair turned to smile at Alphosine. He shrugged. "I don't know. Delilah has something planned, but she didn't share it with me." he squeezed her fingers. "You go to Paris. Have lots of fun shopping."

"Oh Merci!" Alphosine leaned in to give Adair a soft kiss on the cheek. It was one of those high-society cheek-kisses, however she lingered just a moment longer. "You have fun too - go have an adventure."

Adair didn't return the gesture. It wasn't in his culture, and he always felt out of place and phoney when he tried it. He just squeezed Alphosine's fingers back, giving her a fond look. He then looked to her friends. "Umm.. Bon Voyage!" He gave a grin.

Adair stood as the girls chuckled at his meagre command of French. He waved and headed off towards the Administration offices to get their authorization for leave.

-- == == --

Kh't L'nkt was not pleased. His D'rak N'li superiors were noting how quickly the Human situation was unravelling. Instead of sabotaging humanity's changes for admission to the Hegemony, now the Mara were actively investigating looking for outside influences. Kh't L'nkt blamed his personal nemesis - the cadet who with his friends asked too much; looked too much into affairs that didn't concern them; and who could unravel all the work the D'rak N'li have undertaken.

Routines monitoring the various flight plans alerted him to a new avenue. The human's need to trace and track everything in their primitive computers would be their undoing. A flight plan was logged for two of his targets in a small personal craft. If he could not get them in the simulation - he would get them when they were alone in space and outside any protection or intervention.

It would of course need to look like an accident, but disabled and drifting -

not even the Mara's sensors would be able to find their bodies.

With a wicked satisfaction, Kh't L'nkt guided his ship through the folded hyper-dimensions to a translation point outside the atmosphere where he would intercept the small craft.

-- == == --

Adair stepped onto the reinforced ferrocrete landing pad. He had changed into a dark blue polo-style cotton shirt and a pair of black slacks. He had with him a small overnight bag. His UWSF credentials hung from a lanyard around his neck. Following the directions of the landing crew, he ran out towards one of the blunt-nosed Tsiolkovsky landing crafts. The ship's name was clearly marked along the side - 'UWSF Shearwater - SV/TL-087'.

The loading ramp was extended and the hatch fully open. About half the back space was open, the other half fitted with seats allowing a passenger compliment of about 7. There were a set of bags stowed in the back - their pink with white trim clashing with the dull grey metal interior. An open hatch lead from the passenger deck to the bridge, where Delilah sat in a wrap-around chair in the midst of the pre-flight checklist.

"Come on in - where is Al?" she called out when she noticed Adair looking in curiously.

Adair stowed his back, hitting the controls to cycle closed the access ramp and hatch.

"She's going with her friends to Paris instead." He paused and then climbed into the empty co-pilot chair.

"Delilah - how did you manage to get one of the Tsiolkovskys? You flight qualified in it?"

Delilah scoffed. "I've been flying these since I was a wee lass. Remember, my daa's company builds them." She tosses a headset over to Adair. "Did you have any trouble getting our passes?"

"Not at all. I think Sparling wanted to get away too. All of the Maras on base - sticking their noses in. Not to mention all those 'specialists' that Geneva sent in. I think he feels its an invasion of his private space."

Adair reached around to strap himself in. He was familiar with the crafts - having piloted them in Simulations but never hands-on. Delilah continued the flight check-list. Having been cleared for departure, she powered up the contra-gravatics and brought the craft off the surface.

The SF Shearwater glided through the air with none of the rattling indulgence of the old-style rocket launches. The High-Energy Plasmic engine barely thrusting - keeping within limits for atmospheric travel as the boxy craft lifted up into the heavens. Adair had time to enjoy the view - watching the mediterranean sea spread out below and more and more of the Europe and Africa come visible until high nimbus clouds finally obscured some of the details.

Turning on the sensors, Adair helped negotiate the busy low-earth-orbit traffic. Delilah negotiated their route through Unity Station, and then handed off their flight credentials to the United World Gateway Station. Once their course was approved and set, Delilah did a power burn to put them in a Lunar trajectory, and then cut the thrust.

"We have about two hours until course correction. Let's have some fun. Is this your first time in orbit?" Delilah set the various systems on self-guidance, and then cut out the contra-gravatics.

Now on a free-return trajectory towards the moon, they were weightless. Adair was held in by the straps and the slight side pressure of the wrap-around gel-foam seats. The Shearwater was far too small of a craft to have contra-gravatics to provide artificial gravity.

"I've been up to Independence once - before I came to the academy. It was really impressive seeing the old trusses which once held the solar panels - before they switched to Eapo reactors."

Adair followed Delilah's lead and unclipped his restraints. His body started to float freely from the micro-perturbations against the seat. Careful not to hit any of the controls, he twisted his body and pulled himself to the back of the cabin. Bracing his feet against the arms of the command chairs, he cycled the interior hatch and floated into the rear compartment. Delilah floated after him.

Closing the hatch to make sure nothing accidentally flew into the cockpit,

Delilah kicked off the back wall and pulled her body into a ball to spin through the air as she flew over the seats letting out a whoop of delight. Her short hair ebbed and flowed carefree against her head. Adair dove out of the way, twisting his body horizontally between two seats, and then took off after Delilah. Weightlessness was exhilarating.

Eventually, the pair settled down. Panting and out of breath, they floated and just chatted.

"So how did you get access to a landing craft?" Adair was just floating freely, his arms and legs out.

"One of the perks of being a Telford - I suppose." Delilah had hooked her toes under an overhead recessed rail and was floating upside down. "So what is going on with you and Alphosine?" She smiled like the cheshire cat.

"I'm not sure. I find it hard to read women, sometimes." Adair admitted. "She is really easy to talk to - and yet she has all her friends and I don't feel like I fit in with them. They are all nice to me, but I feel like I'm on display or being judged for something."

Delilah listened and nodded. "Go on..."

"I don't know too much about her. I know she comes from a small island - she's really smart and really good with languages."

Delilah's reply is lost as the small landing craft is tossed like a pop-can into a typhoon.

Three distinct impacts sound right after each other, sending the floor flying away and the roof smashing down to impact both of their bodies hard. The lights flare, one of the illumination strips bursting before they all go out. Delilah screams. Dull red lights flicker on, and a hissing noise is audible as the craft continues to spin in a chaotic lateral twist.

Adair tries to right himself to get to Delilah, but is knocked sprawling by a seat-back which swings up errantly and sends him flying against backwards against the rear bulkhead. Glancing over he can see condensation gathering in the seams of a wall plate where the hissing is louder; the ship's structural containment has been compromised.

Concentrating a moment to get used to the torque generated by the twisting room, he flipped to the side wall, and reaching to hand over hand using the seat backs he worked his way to where Delilah was curled up laying sideways on the wall.

"My ankles… I think I broke one." She grimaced.

"We're venting. Let me help you to the cockpit." He gingerly helped untangle Delilah from where her foot had been jammed under the recessed hand-hold. Careful to support her in the shifting micro-gravity they made their way to the front hatch. The controls were black, but an analog panel indicated that there was positive pressure on the other side of the hatch.

Hitting the button to cycle the hatch, nothing happened. Adair quickly then released the manual controls, twisting the large recessed lever to unlock and manually open the door. He gingerly helped Delilah into the cockpit, the air was already getting thin in the back. Before he came through himself, he quickly went to one of the storage lockers, retrieving two of the vacuum suits, and bringing them up to the cockpit.

Bracing himself with the door, he pulled the hatch closed and locked it. Stowing the suits behind the seats, he floated into the co-pilot chair. Ahead of them stars spun in a dizzying array. Every ninety seconds the Earth would twist past - followed thirty seconds later by the moon.

"Did we hit something?" Adair strapped himself in. Most of the panels were dead, or were working on purely internal batteries and not the ships power.

"If we hit something we would have been in much worse shape. No… I don't think so." Delilah concentrated, coaxing what she could from the crippled craft.

"If I was a paranoid person - I'd say this was targeted." Delilah looked over to Adair. "HEPE drive is out. Communications is out. Eapo is out. We are crippled, blind and pretty much invisible."

Delilah exhaled, pain overtaking her. Adair searched under the console, finding an emergency first aid pack, and took out some pain-killers. The pills were only the over-the-counter variety, but it was better than nothing.

-- == == --

Delilah was awoken by the gentle nudge as Adair accidentally bumped her seat as he finished closing the air-lock. Waiting a moment for the air to refill the cabin, he removed his helmet.

"What did you find out? How long have I been out?"

"Maybe a half hour." Adair had used orbit-tape to attach several of the chemical glow-lights to his vac-suit and now was bathed in an eerie green glow. "I got some panels off at the back like you mentioned. We can get at the reaction control systems, but the HEPE was externally mounted on a nacelle - nothing we can do from the inside."

"I really suspect it's fried - even if we could reach it. Any power back there?"

"No - none. There are emergency kits - they have some battery-packs we can steal. We have several vac suits - so there is oxygen. I don't think life support was hit - just that breach in the back. I tried to use that hull foam stuff - but I couldn't seal it."

Delilah shook her head. "That is meant for outside. There are too many cracks between the panels - you'll never be able to seal it from the inside."

Adair nodded.

"I couldn't find anything other than vac-suit communicators. They'd not have anything other than a couple kilometer range - nowhere near what we need to call for help."

Delilah looked out the window. "That view could get me sick." she commented as the stars continued to tumble. "Okay - let's start. We can't call for help. Whoever did this might still be out there."

"I'm not sure - if they were, why didn't they finish us off? This way it looks like we suffered an engine malfunction and drifted off into space. Heck that is if anyone ever does find us. Could we somehow cause the engines to leave a large plasma trail… you know - like a beacon?"

"No. Even if we could get access to the engine - the reactor is gone too."

She looked over and gave a grin. "I'm sorry Adair. I'd get out and push if it would help."

Adair looked at her, and then out the window, watching the Earth, and then the Moon twist by.

"What if we walked for help?"

Delilah gave Adair a funny look. "Did you bump your head? We can't exactly stick our thumb out and hitch a lift."

Adair pointed at the spiralling stars out the window.

"What if we landed?"

"Our HEPE is dead. We would survive reentry, sure - and then slam into the earth at mach 25. And that's if we could get our trajectory back to Earth."

"What about the moon?"

Delilah was silent.

She looked out into space, and then reached for one of the hard-copy emergency books. She flipped to the back page, and then pulled out a zero-G marker to make some calculations.

"Fox… you are BRILLIANT!" She looked at him, her eyes beaming with hope. "We should have enough delta-v to land on the moon. It will be rough - but I don't think I'm getting my deposit back for this crate."

"What do you need me to do?" Adair smiled back.

"I'll do the calculations. Just get ready - You'll be my hands in the back."

-- == == --

It had taken several hours, however working with Adair's help, Delilah managed to jury-rig several of the batteries from the unused vac-suits to provide power to the reaction-control systems. After making a rough operations panel, she returned to the cockpit.

The first order of business was to arrest the uncontrolled spin. Giving orders via suit-comm, Delilah directed Adair to tap on the jets. Each tap caused a momentary jerk to the landing craft. Delilah was strapped into the acceleration couch, however without the Contra-gravitics Adair was forced to brace himself against the bulkheads as the apparent gravity shifted with each application of the control jets until the craft had halted it's spin.

Adair floated to the cockpit to see Delilah drawing with her marker on the curved window.

"I don't have any computer to help me," she explained as calculations marked the side, and the main screen slowly became marked with a tracking chart to allow Delilah to manually determine her rate of descent towards the moon, "I'm going to need to do this manually, and call back the burns."

"That's pretty. When I was up here before, I never saw so many stars" Adair commented.

"Those aren't stars - that's our oxygen out there." Delilah commented without looking up. "Probably bits from our craft too. We're in a small debris field."

"Is it dangerous?"

"No. Not at this relative velocity." She looked back to him. "I'd more worry about slamming into the moon too hard. Or missing it." she looked back at the screen, studying the markings. "If we miss it, our trajectory takes us back to Earth. And then we'd really be boned."

The eagerness and hope that was once in her voice had started to show it's cracks.

Adair floated over, touching his helmet to hers.

"We're going to make it. I have faith in your numbers. You're always right, Delilah."

The wait for the final burn seemed to take forever. Conserving oxygen, they both sat with their vac-suits on and the cockpit devoid of oxygen. Lost in their thoughts, they stared out the window.

"Adair - if you could have told Alphosine how you felt before you left, would you?"

Adair glanced over. "I don't know. I don't think I'd want her to worry about me."

"You'd rather her not know how you felt?" Delilah reached over, and through the thick vac-suit material took Adair's hand.

"I think it would be easier for her not worry."

"She'd worry for you because she cares. And if you cared for her too - I think it's only right that you both admit it. You don't know if you can fly if you don't ever jump."

Adair looked at Delilah through his vac-suit helmet. "That's a funny saying. Delilah - what about you?"

She looked away sharply. "No. There isn't anyone who cares about me."

"We care for you."

"You know what I mean. Like that. I've been too busy to become involved with anyone."

"It's never too late. Maybe when we get back you could try jumping as well."

Delilah chuckled. "Takes two to tango, Fox."

They continued to ride in silence, holding hands.

Delilah looked at the screen, measuring the apparent diameter of the mood and pulling out her marker to make some marks. "It's time. Remember just spurts - not a continuous thrust."

Adair gave Delilah's shoulder a squeeze, and floated to the back. Using the orbit-tape he taped one foot to the wall, and the other to the floor. It was going to be a heck of a ride, and he was tying himself to the mast.

Delilah called back the commands, each thrust causing the craft to jerk against the thrusting. Adair could not watch the moon from the back, but Delilah was front row. The dusty dead grey surface loomed bigger and bigger. Tiny pin-pricks of lights on the horizon indicated several of the regolith mining operations. Unfortunately their trajectory wasn't going close to them.

The Shearwater was heading towards a crater - Delilah using it as a bulls-eye target to help with their landing. Plus the walls of the crater would help her sight her altitude for the final descent.. Most of the thrusting was designed to lose their orbital velocity with corrections to compensate for any twists and torques to keep the ship coming down. There were ample fuel reserves, but Delilah would have one chance at this.

"We're nearly there. If these charts are right, we'll be landing in the Lambert Crater" Delilah called out. On either sides the walls of the crater loomed around them. "One more long burst - and brace yourself. We're going to hit hard." She was already doing the same, tenderly hoping her broken ankles wouldn't hit the floor too hard.

The SS Shearwater came down into the starry lunar night without fanfare. With the reaction engines trying to slow the momentum to the best of their ability, the rectangular craft impacted the uneven floor of the crater moving at about eight meters per second.

The momentum caused the Shearwater to bounce upwards, twisting and trying to impale itself on one of the stubby curved wings. Digging into the regolith like a shovel, the landing craft rolled across the roof, the protruding HEPE engine causing the craft to lurch upwards, coming down hard on the opposite stubby wing.

The weight bends the wing downward, and the Shearwater slides to a halt - laying sideways like a beached whale. Sparks danced over the Eapo reactor and one of the reaction tanks ruptured and started to geyser monopropellant into the air before pressure cut-offs isolated the damage. Rocks and dust dislodged from the impact rolled against the ship, coating it in a small layer of grey dust and pebbles.

Inside, Adair had managed to stay attached to the orbit tape, although he heard a hiss from his one foot. Quickly using the roll of orbit tape still strapped to his waist, he wrapped around the small rip in his suit - sealing it.

He was banged up, and laying on the wall of the craft. His legs were tangled as the wall had become the floor, and his makeshift panel was smashed. They would not be using it again.

"Delilah?" he called up, finally removing himself from the wall and crawling sideways into the cockpit.

Delilah was laying sideways, still strapped to her suit. Her head had impacted the control panel beside her and she was dazed, but conscious.

"Any landing you can walk away from, right?" She looked around. Her half of the cockpit window was buried in the grey dirt. "I think they might take away my wings for this one."

"Only 'cause they are hanging a medal in it's place." Adair grinned, "You did it. You saved us."

"Just be careful out there." Delilah slowly shifted, releasing the restraining belts and very carefully easing herself to an upright position, careful of where she's kneeling on the side computer controls.

"These vac-suits aren't rated for Lunar trips. Just be careful - some of the fractured moon rocks can be as sharp as razors." she nodded down to his foot. "I don't think you have enough orbit-tape if you trip and fall."

"We will be careful." Adair is carefully helping Delilah as she works her way out of the crippled cockpit.

"No. I'm not going." Adair looked at her. "My ankle is busted - even in moon gravity I can't walk. You go and get help."

Adair was about to protest, but Delilah was right. "I'll be very quick." Making sure she was settled in the wall-floor of the landing craft with an ample supply of spare oxygen and batteries from the supplies, he manually cycled the exterior door. He first tossed out three of the helmets. He had jury-rigged the helmet-comm to act as a repeater - allowing him to extend the range of his own suit's communicator. He would leave them like breadcrumbs leading back to the crashed craft. Leaping upwards to catch himself on the lip, Adair lifted his now ⅙ weight body out of the craft.

"Leave the door open - the suits radio signals will travel farther."

Adair carefully knelt on the battered hull of the SS Shearwater. He peered in, and gave a final wave to Delilah, before carefully jumping in a graceful arc to land on the dusty regolith. On the other side of the craft was the long divet dug into the surface when the ship crashed. On this side, the surface was uneven and strewn with boulders the size of volkswagens.

Adair looked around - the ground seemed to just spread out flat in all directions.

"I thought you said we crashed into a crater. It's all flat out here." Adair used the Earth as a sight-guide and started walking away from the ship.

"We are. The moon is small - the horizon is only about two kilometers away. The Lambert crater is nearly thirty wide."

"That means even with these helmets, I won't be able to radio you outside the crater."

"Don't worry about that. We can talk now - tell me a story."

-- == == --

Kh't L'nkt was furious. After disabling the craft, he scanned it to detect that it had sustained major damage, and was crippled and drifting uncontrollably. He watched longer, monitoring the feeble actions of the life-signs within.

As the craft regained control, he watched as it altered course towards the moon. With their radio disabled, there is no way they could call for help. It would be the act of true desperation to try to land on the moon - and yet that's what they did.

Kh't L'nkt had to be more careful here. With Mara ships in lunar orbit, any of his actions would be detected. But he could not the resourceful human go for help. He had one final course of action left to him.

-- == == --

Adair regaled a tale of his youth - growing up in a small town in the rural part of Canada. He was spinning a story about ice skating on the frozen lake in his hometown. The journey was interrupted periodically as Adair had to pause to repair his suit. Sharp lunar rocks ate through the soft rubber soles of his boots, and would also scratch holes in his legs and arms as he brushed past rocks. The orbit-tape would then be wrapped around, making his vac-suit have a mis-mash of bright yellow 'bandaids'.

As he walked, the peak of the crater appeared and started to approach like the lip of an enormous cup spreading from horizon to horizon. Delilah interrupted him.

"You… st'rtin… break-up. Mayb… set those repea… mets." There was a great deal of static on the signal. Adair paused, and then back-tracked several hundred meters.

"Is this better?"

"Yes - I can hear you clearly. What is it like out there?"

Adair looked around - he was in the same field of strewn boulders. Grey and jaggy as far as the eye could see. The kicked up dust had settled on his lower legs of his pants. Even the one-sixth gravity got exhausting to compensate for.

"Oh it's exhilarating. I'm glad I came along." There was only a little sarcasm in his voice.

"I'm glad you came along." Delilah replied after a pause.

Adair withdrew one of the helmets he had brought along, and activated the communicator and repeater. Finding a tall spire of a boulder, Adair quickly jumped up and reached for the spire, swinging his other hand around to leave the helmet perched on the top like a beacon. The extra height would extend his comm-net back towards the crashed Tsiolkovsky. While he was up, Adair thought he saw a glimmer of movement - but that couldn't be. They were supposed to be utterly alone.

Adair continued towards the edge of the crater which quickly loomed over him, continuing his story of the ice rink, how the community would come together to shovel the ice, and help young ones learn to skate. A different time and a different place.

"These cliffs - I'm not sure if I'll be able to scale them." Adair cut his story off again. They had loomed to well over a kilometer high - perhaps even two. It was difficult to tell at this angle. They started with a gentle arc of fractured ground, but quickly rose to a near vertical surface. The ground also had intermixed from the crevasases ancient lava flows - now a glossy sharp black rock resembling obsidian.

"I might need to try to find another way, Delilah." Adair paused.

"Delilah, are you receiving me?"

He turned back towards the ship, but just saw featureless rocks. Pursing his lips he looked back, and then looked down.

Taking a large rounded rock, he lifted it high over his head and brought it down hard on an elongated shard of lava-rock. It cracked and flew away with little black shards flying everywhere.

Retrieving the long shard, he used orbit-tape to wrap around the base so he didn't cut the gloves of his suit, and with his makeshift 'sword', he started back towards the helmet.

As he approached the other helmet, Adair felt the hairs on the back of his neck prickle. He crouched behind a boulder, and drew the second helmet. This time he activated not just the communications, but also the camera setting it to record and send the feed. Reaching up, he perched the helmet on the rock, and set his internal camera to stream the feed to a small window displayed inside his helmet.

Gripping his sword, he started the final hundred meters towards the other helmet.

"Adair... Los'... Coming in? ...Adair... signa... " he started to hear faintly over the comms.

Adair didn't respond, creeping closer to the first helmet. He finally was close enough to see it.

The remains of the helmet were scattered over the top of the boulder - it looked like it had been ripped apart as if someone had peeled it like an explosive onion.

Adair suddenly saw a quick shift of the shadows in the relayed camera image. It was gone too quickly before he could focus on it. He was not alone.

His heart started to race as he withdrew the final helmet. He would have one shot at this - otherwise he would lose any advantage he had. And he had no idea of what he was up against - only that they were better armed than him and stalking him.

He turned covered the front, and turned on the helmet's light. He then flicked the 'emergency transmit' mode and with an elongated bowling motion, heaved the helmet high up into space.

The helmet spun, it's light making a strobing effect as the comm-signals were filled with a harsh repeating emergency signal. Adair crouched and watched the monitor, turning off the comms in his own helmet.

There - movement.

In the slow-motion of one-sixth gravity Adair sprinted back towards the - whatever it was.

It was vaguely humanoid, only standing about four feet tall. It had four arms, with a strange crest or 'wing' between the arms - but that might have just been the strange black shiny suit it was wearing. All of it's appendages ended in four-fingered elongated claws, and the helmet had another strange crest which was articulated and moved as the creature moved.

It followed the lazy arc taken by the spinning helmet, and raising a hand holding a very weapon-like shape he fired. There was no laser beam - no puff of energy. The weapon discharge wasn't visible to human eyesight, and when the mesons charge phased into real-space and collided with the helmet, it ripped it apart as effective as any explosive charge, shredding the helmet like a blooming onion.

Adair thought he had the advantage, but when he was more than an arm's length away, the creature twisted, and shot it's weapon. The obsidian sword shattered, razor sharp shards of black glass shredding the side and leg of Adair's suit.

Adair stumbled, feeling the lancing pain and icy cold shooting through his side and leg. He fell to the ground, his hand holding the stump of what was his weapon.

Kh't L'nkt stood triumphant over Adair. Victory was his. He watched as the air misting out of the various slices in Adair's suit take on a faintly pink hue. He lowered his meson blaster, and reached to key his communicator and translator.

"There will be no saving you this time." The voice was mechanical and computerized as the alien translator switched his words into English. Behind the words, the native language of the alien was abrupt with numerous clicks and low chirrs. There was no mistaking the tone.

"You have swarted me for the last time."

The short creature stepped forward and loomed over Adair. Adair gasped, rolling to his side to try to look up, but all he saw was the helmet and black suit the vaguely bat-like creature wore.

Kh't L'nkt bent over, taking Adair's helmet in his small but powerful hands, and lifted Adair up. He clenched with his one hand crushing the camera and comm unit. "We can't have any evidence - can we?" the electronic voice sneered.

"I will watch you die."

Adair feebly tried to raise the broken blade up, but it is knocked aside by the lower set of arms.

"Resistant to the end. And now I get to watch you die." It's claw-like fingers curled, and Adair heard a sudden hiss as his helmet was breached.

"LET HIM GO YOU TWISTED FREAK!"

Delilah lunched out from behind, bringing a panel from the HEPE housing down hard on the back of the alien's head. The hull alloy bent and the creature dropped Adair into the dust.

Delilah fell to a knee, her broken ankle unable to support any weight. She looked up as Kh't L'nkt turned towards her, raising his firearm.

"Oh good! You save me the trouble of hunting you down. Die now!" lifting the blaster to fire.

Delilah closed her eyes and clenched. Nothing happened.

She opened her eyes to see the alien looking down. Three of it's claws held it's small chest - the tip of a broken glass blade protruding. It's helmet looked up at Delilah as the blaster fell from it's claw, and it fell sideways to the ground.

"Not today." rasped Adair, and then collapsed. His breathing was laboured and shallow.

Kh't L'nkt reached over, activating the fail-safes in his suit. Delilah ignored the alien body, scrambling over to Adair. The alien suit shimmered, and then twisted and folded itself into the inaccessible hyper-dimensions leaving no evidence. Except the dropped meson blaster.

"Fox… talk to me. Oh God!" Delilah saw the pinkish mist was slowing - there wasn't much oxygen left in his suit. Adair looked pale and motionless inside the cracked helmet. Taking the orbit-tape from his waist, she liberally wrapped it around the helmet, and then started to work on his arms, body and legs.

"Talk to me. Talk to me dammit!" She pulled up his suit comp, but it was flashing error messages. In his fight with the alien, his suit had gotten damaged.

Delilah took several deep breaths, calming herself down and filling her lungs. She then reached to her own suit, unhooking the oxygen reprocessor feed and snaking the short hose towards his suit.

It wouldn't reach.

inwardly cursing, Delilah stretched her body out over Adairs, laying across his. She reached down, now able to hook the life-giving hose to his suit. She continued to hold her breath, watching Adair through the touching visors.

Adair suddenly convulsed, and took a breath. Delilah smiled, very slowly exhaling. She had a couple breaths of air in her own suit.

Adair tried to speak, but his comms were down. Delilah just smiled back at him. He reached down, feeling her arm, and tracing it down to the life-giving umbilical attaching both of them. He gave Delilah a thankful nod.

-- == == --

Two of the Tsiolkovsky landing crafts were accompanied by a much sleeker looking Mara shuttle as well a bulbous looking Chinese landing shuttle as they flew down towards the lunar surface. The four crafts flew over the crashed landing craft, and then followed the pathway until they slowed over the two prone suits laying in the lunar dust. The ships carefully landed a short distance away.

In full lunar excursion vac-suits, grey and cobalt, and armed with zero-g variants of the gauss carbines, U.W.S.F. marines charged out along with the crimson and equally armed Chinese Republic Marines. The bodies did not move.

The lead Marine held his hand up, the assembled troops halted as they scanned around. The group was joined by a holographic projection of the Mara, who looked around and communicated over the comm's with the rest of the soldiers. The lead marine slung his rifle and ran to the bodies.

Delilah and Adair concentrated on breathing slowly. Both of their suits had several micro-tears and the orbit-tape had run out. They were savouring the time the had left when Adair spotted points of light moving. What seemed like an eternity later, before a marine knelt over them. Through his helmet, Adair saw Professor Sparling looking down at him.

"Howdy, Sir." Adair mouthed - his comm's broken.

"They are alive," Professor Sparling stood back up. "Get them to the shuttle and to immediate medical attention." He then looked over at the strange looking hand-weapon discarded nearby.

-- == == --

Undetected, even by the advance Mara sensors, sat the D'rak N'li interdiction cutter. At the triggering of the fail-safe, the craft had gathered all of the recent comm and intercepted video and audio evidence before sending a high-priority hyper-net squirt back to the D'rak N'li command.

Command knew of Kh't L'nkt failure. Command knew that the humans now had concrete evidence against outside influence. Command knew it was only a matter of time before the Mara would bring the Kh't L'nkt Collective to a Patron Hegemony Constituent, a senior race within the Hegemony who would punish them for breaking the codified regulations for dealing with an Unconstrained Collective - the Hegemony term for a race who was not yet part of the Hegemony.

Command knew that drastic measures were needed. Measures that would look like outright thousand to one happenstance, and take care of the Mara while they were at it. There would be an investigation, but by that point the Kh't L'nkt could remove all traces of itself from the sphere of Humanity.

Command knew.

8

The Hegemony was not very forthcoming with details of it's inner working, however over the last decade through various dealings both with the Mara and with the scant dealings with other races, some details have been able to be pieced together.

The Hegemony is highly hierarchical in structure, and it is very difficult for a species to travel between the hierarchies. There exists a culture of restricted information and inclusion which restricts societies in the lower levels from knowing the powers, responsibilities and requirements of those above them. There is also an inherent distrust - however that could be a misperception due to how other races react towards Humanity, which is at the lowest of these levels.

Races which are not part of the Hegemony are classified as the Unconstrained Collective. There may be translation issues causing actual titles to not be a true translation, but a close approximation. There are several major types of the Unconstrained Collective, roughly grouped into societies which are not yet space-borne, societies which are space-borne and are close to being considered for membership in the Hegemony, and societies which have been offered membership but have refused. Humanity falls into the second category. It is interesting to note there is scant details on the third - those races would be almost certainly labelled as enemies to the Hegemony. Earth has never had any contact with any other Unconstrained Collective - of any type.

The majority of races, including the Mara, belong to a group labeled the Transitory Hegemony Constituent. These races are expected to follow directives given by the Hegemony without question and without recourse. There are strict rules which guide their interactions with other societies based on level.

The Hegemony is run by a group of societies referred to as the Patron Hegemony Constituents. These races are the ones which determine the rules and direction of the Hegemony. Their membership is tightly controlled, and reports estimate that throughout the entire galaxy there are only perhaps two dozen races which are at this level. Humanity has never met a Patron Hegemony Constituent, nor are we even aware of any species of this classification.

There is a near mythological final level. Only referred to as the Nadir Hegemony Sovereign, this single race is reputedly one of the oldest in the galaxy - perhaps the universe. The Nadir Hegemony, if they do exist, would represent a species hundreds of thousands, if not millions of years old, and would have unimaginative power and influence.

"In-Depth study on Alien Relations"
Fleet Admiral Edward Melara (ret), UWSF - 2030

Adair remembered his head throbbing - the grip in his chest as their shared air barely kept them alive - the icy cold that had numbed his side and arm from the lack of insulation the orbit-tape provided. He thought he had dreamed about stars moving overhead, and Professor Sparling coming to wish him farewell.

He felt pressure on his chest and right arm. A dull pain was lower just below his wrist, and there was something strapped around his head. His left hand also had pressure of a different sort.

"Are you awake?" Alphosine lent over the hospital bed, still holding Adair's hand.

Adair blinked and tried to move, but his muscles were weak and aching. He blinked again, trying to resolve the blurry mess of colours. The pale green walls of the infirmary came into view. Alphosine was floating beside Adair, her hand firmly holding his left hand as he lay on a thin platform that formed a body-contoured bed affixed to one wall. Several machines continued monitoring and caring for Adair. The air had the taste of recycled 'space air'.

"Where am I?" Adair's throat was dry, and his voice muffled through a form-fitting oxygen mask. He was laying inside a sac which attached him firmly to the bed. Alphosine was floating free, with her toes slipped under a recessed grip.

"You're on Gateway Station. Delilah is here too - and Boyd."

Adair smiled weakly and laid back.

"How?"

"It was the Mara - I don't know too much. They were tracking you, and then alerted the UWSF command when you crashed."

Adair glanced over at Alphosine, his eyes steely.

"We were attacked."

Alphosine floated close, her voice serious.

"I know. Everyone knows - but there is a big political cover-up. Officially it was written off as a manufacturing defect so it didn't affect Delilah or your flight rank. The Mara are involved - and same with senior command. Professor Sparling is…"

"What am I, Cadet Fuluhea?"

Professor Sparling floated into the isolated room. He wasn't wearing his standard teachers dress, but instead had a UWSF spacer's jumpsuit on, with the rank Chief Master Sergeant on his shoulder.

"I would like to speak with Cadel Fox alone, please. You are dismissed."

Alphosine squeezed Adair's hand and then floated out of the room. Professor Sparling floated closer. Adair looked at the Professor and tried to speak.

"No, Adair. Not yet." He hooked his feet under the same restraint and floated close, holding onto the side of the bed with practiced ease.

"There are going to be people who want to talk to you. The Mara included. Vice-Admiral Rees has done what he can to protect you and Cadel Telford. This goes very deep, and we cannot talk freely here." His eyes looked grave.

"I'm not where where we can talk anymore. There is great pressure to cover this up. The official story is that this crash was a technical malfunction. Cadet Telford is being most defiant - understandable as it casts the blame on her father's company. You will need to help with her - There is more."

He shifts closer, whispering.

"There is no evidence of the attack. Everything is being suppressed by the Mara."

A memory came back to Adair.

"Helmet recorder…"

"Your helmet recorder was damaged, and there was no means to retrieve any data."

"Not mine - nearby - left a helmet recording."

The professor stopped, his mind going quickly. "Who else knows?"

"No one."

He nodded. "Keep it that way, Fox. You can't tell anyone outside the military. Earth might be under attack - and if the Mara has been keeping it from governments. Or even worse - the governments involved with the cover-up - we will need to get that evidence to protect the Earth."

Adair turned to face the professor. "A little melodramatic?"

Professor Sparling chuckled and nodded. "Perhaps. But that helmet, and a small device I found might be the only concrete evidence we have. I will report this to the Vice-Admiral - and go retrieve that helmet. I need you to convince Cadet Telford to also cooperate until we have more proof."

Adair tried to raise his hand to salute, but he couldn't. Professor Sparling chuckled and reached over to release the restraints. "Here you go." He then straightened up, giving Adair a salute.

"You did a brave thing on the Moon, Cadet Fox. You kept a level head and came back, and might have found the key to understand what is going on."

Adair saluted back, the tubes floating in the zero gravity. "Thank you, Sir"

-- == == --

There was not much privacy in the hospital node, however as they were the only 'guests' at the moment, Adair and Delilah moved from their tiny private rooms to the main central room. Adair's strength was quickly coming back to him - it did not take much effort to move in microgravity - and he enjoyed seeing his friends.

"So you left your Mother standing in the rain?" Adair couldn't believe the story.

Boyd floated upside-down. He had the habit of always inverting his stance just to try to draw attention to himself whenever he could. "Well, I got the MESH that you guys had crashed on the Moon."

Delilah bristled. It was obvious she vehemently objected to her family name being stained to cover up the alien attack.

"And we were at this family picnic - in my honour. It was overcast, but that's what we get for going to Central Park in the middle of November. Anyways I MESHed the closest transport, skimmed over to Mojave and caught the next shuttle up here to Gateway."

Delilah floated over to give Boyd a large hug.

"And we both thank you for it."

Alphosine was quiet as she always tended to be whenever Boyd and Delilah were around. She floated near the side, glancing occasionally at Adair until he caught her eyes before looking away with a slight blush.

"This has got to be bigger than when the simulation was hacked." Boyd was caught up in conspiracy theories, and as much as it bothered Adair and Delilah - they agreed they couldn't tell him the truth. Not yet.

"No Boyd - I'm pretty sure it will be classes as normal when we return." Adair said, his tone carefully neutral. After a moment, he gave Delilah a pointed look.

"Yeah - I wouldn't be surprised if we have to write an essay on the geological features of the lunar regolith." her tone was still bitter.

One of the UWSF midshipman wearing the familiar cobalt blue jumpsuits entered the medical cupola. "Your shuttle will be arriving in an hour - time for you lot to get back ground-side"

-- == == --

Adair and Delilah knew it was only a matter of time before they ended up here. While most of the academy had heard about the crash - details were scant and each story was more impressive than the last.

Other cadets could be kept in the dark, and while there was no official requirement, when Agiprom Intirum Ciltra summoned Adair and Delilah for a private conference, they could not refuse. In the decade since first contact, with the exception of the initial private meetings between world leaders and the Mara, no representative had ever been in the presence of more than one Mara at a time.

Agiprom Intirum Ciltra was joined by Agiprom Intirum Citral and Agiprom Prime Lalrit in the interview room with Adair and Delilah. Outside, Marines belonging to the Diplomatic Security Corp stood along USWF Marines providing security for the private talk.

Agiprom Prime Lalrit was tall, even for a Mara. His features were deeply chiseled, and his head-crest had some frills and holes, as if it had been eroded away. He was silent, but his eyes were always watching with burning intensity. His uniform was also distinct from the other Agiprom Intirum, and even from the uniform Adair remembered seeing Agiprom Prime Centri wearing.

Agiprom Intirum Ciltra conducted most of the interview, with interjections from Agiprom Intirum Citral.

"The official story is that the UWSS Shearwater suffered technical malfunction causing your crash-landing on the satellite surface."

Adair was more reserved this time in dealing with the Mara. "You are correct, Agiprom Intirum."

"Does your own observations bear out this conclusion, Cadet?"

Adair glanced at Delilah. "We do not have any observations to add, Agiprom Intirum." His tone was carefully neutral.

Agiprom Intirum Citral advanced a step - his seven foot frame imposing as all four arms came out. "Our analysis detected depleted nucleonic degradation to your hull - focused on the communication and motive power units!"

"Perhaps you could make the analysis available to our technicians - it would help pin-point the source of the malfunction." Adair had a slight edge to his voice.

Ciltra raised a hand to motion Citral to calm down. "Unfortunately our technical readouts are not compatible with human systems. There were no artifacts recovered from the Moon that you are aware of?" Three pairs of large black eyes focused on Adair.

"I'm sorry, Agiprom Intirum. I was unconscious at the time. I cannot comment on what may have been taken from the Moon."

Citral's head crests vibrated, making a sound vaguely like a rattlesnake. Ciltra raised his hand again, and continued questioning.

"Have you ever been contacted, or have contact with any other Hegemony race?"

Adair smiled bitter-sweetly back. "That would not be permitted under the rules of the Hegemony Visitation and Monitoring. I'm sorry, Agiprom Intirum - I don't have any information for you."

Citral reached out, grabbing Adair by the uniform, and lifted him into the air. When he spoke it was a guttural harsh native tongue, before accusing Adair, "You were attacked, and you know it. Tell us WHO did this!"

Agiprom Prime Lalrit spoke a harsh phrase in the Mara language, and then made a ceremonial bow. Citral dropped Adair like his hands were holding hot coals, and then forced himself to make the same formal bow. Ciltra bowed and spoke.

"Our apologies, Cadet Adair, Cadet Telford. Please excuse the out-burst - these are times filled with high emotion. We have no more questions."

The three Mara bowed their heads, and it was clear that there was going to be no more details forthcoming.

9

The Exo-Solar Long-Range Reconnaissance Platform-3, or ELRP-3 was never meant to be fully manned, however had minimal support functions for crews who were on-station for housekeeping and maintenance. In a high orbit over Neptune, it was one of the farthest manned base and could only be serviced by ships with the recently available FT-Hop drive.

The ELRP program was designed to provide monitoring of the Oort cloud and beyond. It consisted of a series of satellites deployed both within the Neptunian system and at the trojan points along Neptune's orbit along with the manned platform. The raw data from the satellite network was processed, compressed, and encrypted at each satellite and forwarded to the platform. The ELRP would then send the encoded transmissions using it's high-gain antenna to Earth. Each transmission took 246 minutes.

The UWSS Moscow, hull registry SS/D-03, was launched in 2024 after two years of construction. One of the earliest Archimedes-class ships, the SS Moscow did not have FT-Hop capability and thus had a very limited operational range of 10 months before a resupply was required. The ship had a crew complement of 48 and carried an additional 30 marines. Standard on Archimedes-class ships were both an emergency combat hospital and research labs.

The initial data-packets from the ELRP-3 contained data corruptions and anomalies which raised concern on Earth. The ELRP program was just coming online, but any immediate action was overshadowed by the SS Enterprise catastrophe. The UWSF Command needed to get a presence on site, and with no FT-Hop capable ship unavailable, the SS Moscow was redirected from it's mission in the Jupiter system to investigate the strange readings at the platform. Stretched to the limits of it's range, the SS Moscow took 6 months to reach the Neptune system via conventional plasmic drive.

The final transmissions came from the SS Moscow just after rendez-vous with the Exo-Solar Long-Range Reconnaissance Platform. The imaging data included a static-filled image of the platform which had a black crystalline substance covering the outside, like a mold slowly covering a rock. The transmission also contained audio logs which were also static-filled and heavy corrupted. The technicians managed to recover the following audio segment, "... don't touch it. Captain! I see movement. We are not alone!". There were no further transmissions from the SS Moscow.

The Secretary-General of the United World Council contacted the President of the United States and the President of the People's Republic of China - the two other independent space-faring nations. The Chinese had no ships available, however President Devon Wolfe authorized the use of the military. The USAS Texas SDD-2, an american Hercules-class destroyer was sent on a follow-up mission to discover the fate of the SS Moscow and the ELRP-3 station. Using it's FT-Hop drive, the USAS Texas was able to enter the Neptunian system 15 days after the loss of transmission from the SS Moscow. Two further days were required to carefully recon the system before approaching the last known coordinates of the missing ship. There were no signs of the SS Moscow, and the orbital platform was reduced to a skeletal backbone structure of empty aluminum trusses.

After 12 weeks of intensive search operations, the following details were ascertained. Twisted wreckage from a Sun Tzu class strike craft was found on Nereid. The wreckage had been disrupted at a molecular level causing 74% of the main superstructure to have been destroyed. There were also traces of cloud disruptions in the Neptune upper cloud deck and traces of elements not known to be present in the Neptunian atmosphere. Computer simulations back on Earth indicated a potential source of an Archimedes sized ship entering the atmosphere. There was no recovered wreckage from the SS Moscow, nor any trace of the 80 missing humans.

``Joint Commission on the Neptune Incident''
UWSF/USSF - 2026

The bridge illumination was subdued giving the room a warm autumn hue, primarily due to the main view-screen. Unearthly swirls of reds, yellows, oranges and colours and patterns which seemed to defy description filled the screen. Eddies and whirls larger than continents interspersed with lightning storms with bolts of electricity the size of cities played over the turbulent skin of Jupiter causing shifting colours to dance throughout the walls of the bridge .

Commander Christina Grigg leant forward in the command chair, mesmerized by the visage for a moment, before turning to the officer to the right.

"Lieutenant Telford - give me a full sweep. What are we up against?"

Delilah acknowledged the order "Yes, Captain" with a professional neutral tone. She had fully recovered, and with classes resumed, even managed to leave the ire of the ruse mostly behind her. She looked down, her fingers a blur as she ran a multi-phase full spectrum active EMS scan of the jovian system. The holo-screens danced with tiny readouts, their ship's projected course overlaid tracing pathways through multiple overlaid colours from the readouts from different spectrums of electromagnetic radiation.

"Captain. I'm receiving a signal. It's faint and repeating, but human." Alphosine spoke from the console on the far opposite wall. Christina turned to face her.

"Elaborate please."

Adair had been silent the entire time. He was standing to the left and slightly behind the commander's chair. As Alphosine delved into the readings, he took the opportunity to stride across the bridge, looking over her shoulder at the readouts.

"It's a repeating signal. I'm decrypting now - it has an American military transponder." Alphonsine worked on the signal, trying to coax more details from the faint corrupted signal.

Adair had also fully recovered. Cadets were still slightly wary around him - which suited him fine. After the repeated private meetings with the Mara, Adair was viewed as either blessed or cursed. Watching over Alphosine's shoulder for a moment for a moment, he spoke out. "Edgar - display the

Jovian system. Overlay source of signal."

The artificial intelligence operating the ship's MESH responded in a rich male voice from the bridge, "Acknowledged, Lieutenant Commander"

The main viewscreen changed, instantly the room brightening from the Jovian cloud deck to a graphical representation of their orbital path. Jupiter was represented by an arc at the top of the display, with the orbital traces of Io, Europa and Ganymede being traced out in different coloured arcs. The ship had already passed the orbit of Callisto and was following a gentle curving arc in an elliptical orbit around Jupiter.

The signal was highlighted to be coming from a very low orbit around Io. There is no way the orbit would be stable - the orbital decay until the source of the signal could be measured in days or hours. There was heavy static and interference on the signal.

"That's strange," Christina commented, leaning forward. "I would have figured that any activity out here would be around Europa. Aren't there a couple base in the Jupiter system?"

Delilah turned her back from her scanning, and spoke up with an almost encyclopedic tone. "Well, there is the G-3 station at Callisto - the Galileo Galilei Ground Installation. That's joint US and United World. There is also the Clarke Station in Europa orbit. But neither of them have anything other than unmanned probes around Io."

Christina thought on this for a moment, then nodded and spoke to the helmsman.

"Okay. Helm, take us in. Set a course to orbit Io - let's investigate."

Something twigged at the back of Adair's head. That felt wrong - not to mention that the entire simulation had not yet revealed its 'surprise'. "Commander, a word?"

Christina frowned as Adair did not countermand her order, but it was apparent he had issues. She looked at him, but Adair nodded towards the conference hall. Christina sighed and nodded. "Very well." She looked at the helmsman. "Calculate that course," and stood up, walking towards the ship's lecture theatre.

As the helms officer started calculating the course correction, Adair glanced across the bridge to catch the eyes of Delilah. "Can you join us please?" The rest of the crew watched on while he followed her into the lecture hall.

-- == == --

The lecture theatre on the SS Beijing was spacious enough for the entire crew to gather if need be. Half wrapping around the front portion of the bridge, it slightly sloped downward towards the display podium. There were small half-tables in front of the rows of seats which all faced the center podium in large sweeping semi-arcs. The lighting was recessed in the ceiling and kept at a low level. The holo-display behind the podium was in standby mode and displayed the ship's logo, the ships title "UWSS Beijing - SS/D-10" and its motto quoting Ambrose Redmoon, 'Courage is not the absence of fear, but rather the judgement that something else is more important than fear.'

Christina stalked halfway towards the podium and then stopped. She was not happy at being questioned on her first command.

"What is the meaning of this, Fox? You showboating again?" There was emotion and indignation in her voice at being interrupted when she was clearly in command. "If you recall - the last time I listened to you, we lost."

Adair remained calm. He approached Christina and looked her in the eyes. "Please, just listen. Delilah - can you pull your readings up on the display there. Bring up the charged ion radiation around Io."

Christina turned around as Delilah went up to the holo-display controls, and patched her bridge terminal into this room. After a moment the room dimmed and the holo-display flared into life.

The orbital status was displayed along with the mysterious signal in low Io orbit. Delilah hit several buttons and the entire orbital track of Io flared into life - angry red glow which seemed to ebb and twist with some unseen mathematics. Around Io itself, the haze intensified, the red shifting into a yellow then white glow which made Io difficult to look at.

"The signal is orbiting someplace around five thousand kilometers around Io - at the limit of the Hill Sphere. It's right in the middle of the massive cloud of super charged particles from Jupiter's magnosphere."

"But the Beijing - she has Meissner Shields. Shouldn't that protect us from the ionization?" Christina's tone was starting to drop.

Adair looked to Delilah to answer this one. She thought for a moment.

"She does, but the charged radiation is magnitudes stronger than the Beijing's standard rating. It's outside the design specifications. We could survive for minutes, but it would cause havoc with our systems."

The intra-ship comm chimed, and Alphosine joined in.

"Excuse me Captain, I've managed to isolate the signal. It's a distress signal from the USAS Pioneer."

Christina frowned. She looked at the comm and listened to Alphosine with a 'what is it now?' look on her face. She looked back to Adair, her eyes steely and serious. "I wonder if there other cadets manning the Pioneer. Adair - can you come up with any ways to rescue them?"

Suddenly the lighting in the room shifted. Recessed lights flickered from dull pale white to an angry red, and a repeating warning tone sounded. The looked at each other for a moment.

"Oh what now! Get back to the bridge." Christina frowned and commanded Adair and Delilah before pushing past them and returning to her command.

-- == == --

The bridge lighting also had a red cast to it, and a short bar under the main screen glared back red angrily into the room like a baleful eye. The main viewscreen was displaying a long-range sensor feed. There was an indeterminate reading from the far side of Jupiter on a fast closing trajectory - it's trajectory thumbing the nose at newton and gravitational mechanics.

Delilah studied the path of the unknown target, commenting aloud, "Look at the stupid waste of energy to close on that trajectory. Such a reckless stupid waste."

Christina re-took her command chair, looking down to Adair as he returned to the bridge last and paused at the front of the bridge, turning to regard the sensor readout silhouetted against the main viewscreen.

"Well.. we don't know it is hostile, however it can't be a coincidence."

Christina commented, assessing the situation. She hit one of the buttons on her command chair. "Warm up the weapons. Prepare the torpedos and all Sun-Tzu's for launch."

Adair didn't look back as he asked, "Delilah - what about one of the Tsiolkovsky's. Could one of the landing craft take the radiation?"

She thought about this a moment and nodded. "Only barely. They are smaller though - they would be thrown around like crazy. It would be insane to suggest it."

Adair looked back to Captain Grigg. She gave the look back, searching Adair's eyes. Words were not exchanged for a moment, the exchange lit by the flashing red warning signals. Other bridge officers held their breath, not wanting to make a sound.

"Lieutenant-Commander Fox." Christina started with a level tone, "If I forbid this absurd folly of yours, what are the chances that you'd listen to reason?"

Adair looked at the screen, then back at his commanding officer. "Someone needs to rescue the crew of the Pioneer."

Christina let out a long sigh. "Go! Just remember that I tried to stop you." Adair sprinted past, heading out the door at the rear of the bridge to the closest elevator to the hanger deck. Christina turned to the helms. "Plot an intercept with whatever that is. Let's see if we can buy some time for Captain Screwball."

Alphosine made a little sound from the communications station. "Communications will be impossible through that ionization. We won't be able to follow him." There was obvious concern in her voice, but she turned back to look at her console.

Delilah on the other hand was practically out of her seat. She looked right at Christina and raised her hand.

With another sigh, Christina turned to look at Delilah. She studied her face. "Your skills would be better suited staying on the Beijing." Delilah didn't answer back, but her expression carried the determination of where she would prefer to be. "FINE! Go!" She turned away so she didn't have to watch Delilah stand and sprint after Adair.

Christina turned back to the main screen and hit the all-comm button. "This is Commander Griggs. We are about to engage an unknown force - presumed hostile. All hands to combat stations."

-- == == --

The Immersion Room had been cleared for a week before the simulations had resumed. The rumours surrounding the crash of the shuttle on the moon were dying down, and any official investigations into the incident were stalled by political interference from the Mara. Further investigations into the sabotage of the simulations had also ended up with dead-ends. Technicians could recover no evidence of technical tampering and Elisha retained no logs of the activity. After reviewing the findings from the independent technical auditors, the board of directors and Director-General of UWESCD herself had cleared the school to continue using the simulations.

Professor Sparling did not find any of that comforting as he turned angrily to the base commandant.

"Henry - you promised me that we'd keep those kids safe! You and I know that something squirrely is going on, and those political puppets are busy playing charades. Why did you let those kids go back in there." Sparling was angry.

The holodisplays provided most of the illumination on Vice-Admiral Henry-Joseph Rees. The lights in the control room had been dimmed, and even in the dancing coloured display from the screens, Henry's face had additional deep set lines from his long bureaucratic meetings with his superiors, with the United World Education, Science and Cultural Directorate Director-General, with the independent technical auditors and with the Hegemony representatives - the Mara.

"The technicians had cleared it. And the Director-General ordered their use. We can't simply shut down the school - we need to get those kids up in the skies."

"I don't care if the order came from God himself - it's my cadets who are in danger in there."

"Chief Master Sergeant!"

Professor Sparling stiffened at attention. Vice-Admiral Rees continued, "I have every intention of protecting this school and every soul in it."

"Then pull the plug, Sir. On the Simulation… On Elisha. Get them out." Sparling looked back up at the screen. "We can do this the old fashioned way."

Vice-Admiral Rees sighed wearily and leant forward on the consoles, regarding the bay of bodies on the slab-like tables below. "I would if I could. Regulations prevent any cadets from serving on active vessels. Until they graduate - this is all we have."

-- == == --

The landing bay was a hive of activity. Teams were loading and checking the munitions on the three Sun-Tzu strike craft. On the other half of the bay, the three Tsiolkovsky Landing Crafts were powered up with Marines milling outside. Adair ran over, and one of the flight officers tossed him a set of Vacc-Armour.

"Lieutenant-Commander - we're reporting as ordered by Commander Griggs" the leader of the marines saluted.

"We only need half of you, divided up among the craft. We need space for bringing back the survivors." Adair said as he started pulling on the hard-shell suit which would protect him in the case of a breach and provide additional protection against the heavy radiation. Adair raised his voice to the flight-deck chief. "I'll also need two of your best pilots."

"You already got that, fox." Delilah grinned, running up and taking a set of Vacc-Armour that another flight officer provides. "You think I'm going to let you fly this without a wingman - you're crazy."

Adair looked over and smiled at Delilah. "Thanks D. You are the best."

"Maybe in her own mind," interjected Boyd as he joined the group, "But if you really want to succeed you'll need a Johnson." He smirked and caught a helmet thrown his way. Boyd was already dressed in a marine-style Vacc-Armour which had additional hardpoints for attaching weapons and provided a sleeker multi-faceted silhouette to the large black man. "Toss me one of those bad-boys" he motioned to one of the Marines.

Boyd caught the ruggedized carbine tossed his way and expertly attached it his rear-shoulder hardpoint, proclaiming "Boh-ya" before he pulled his more heavily armoured helmet over his head. Lights on the helmet came alive, and sensor clusters on the sides of the helmet came to life giving an almost techno-organic feel to the militarized Vacc-Armours.

Adair nodded, and motioned towards the Marines. "Two - Two - and Two. You will come in each of our shuttles - keep the shuttles decompressed and make sure everyone is strapped in." He looked over to Delilah to share a moment before continuing, "The rest of you, be prepared for when we come in. We'll likely have injured and need assistance moving the worst to med-bay"

Delilah smiled back through semi-domed helmet. Like Adair, her Vacc-Armour was designed for pilots, and was more organic and bubble-like compared against the marine sets. She winked at Adair and gave him the thumbs up before reaching up to give Boyd a hearty slap on his shoulder as she runs past towards her shuttle followed by her marines.

Boyd grinned back at Delilah, taking a swipe at returning the playful hit, but missing. He turned and clapped Adair on the shoulder. "You just try to keep up with me." and nodded to the other marines. "Let's roll."

Adair looked back with a serious look. "This isn't a game, Boyd!"

Boyd paused and turned around - his features lost behind the helmet, but Adair could imagine his carefree grin, "Uhh… Yeah it is." he turned and reached for the top of the hatch to swing himself into the third Tsiolkovsky landing craft.

-- == == --

The three Sun-Tzu strike craft launched from the fore-facing launch bay while Adair, Delilah and Boyd flew the Tsiolkovsky from the taller but narrower rear bay. The strike craft maintained a triangular pattern around the crew transports until the interference from the turbulent charged particles required them to turn back.

As the winged strike craft banked and altered their course, streamers of charged ions interacting with the Meissner Shields left an ultraviolet glow which spilt occasionally into the visible light spectrum, leaving dancing violet streamers behind the craft.

The heavily shielded Tsiolkovskys continued towards the stricken USAS Pioneer. It too left ultraviolet and purple streamers behind it as it orbited through the heavy radiation belts caused by the Jovian giant.

Meanwhile, the SS Beijing altered course, plotting to intercept the intruder. Superheated plasma lept from it's drives as it burned at maximum acceleration to attempt to match the speed and maneuverability of the incoming craft. A long trail of blue and white plasma made the ship look like it was a tiny silver flare, with the thousand kilometer trail curving as it interacted with the massive magnetosphere of Jupiter.

-- == == --

Adair reached up to turn off the channel with the SS Beijing. Alphosine may have been able to clear up the static interference coming over the channels, but he had his hands full trying to keep the bucking craft on a course towards the drifting American destroyer.

'It's better that she stayed behind' he thought to himself. "I'd hate myself if anything happened to her." he mused aloud.

"I should hope so." Delilah's voice crackled from the open channel. "Hey Fox… how about you concentrate on flying, and leave the daydreaming behind."

"When you are done flirting - will you guys look at that?" Boyd chimed in. The craft drew nearer to the crippled ship. "Why is it yellow? I didn't think the Americans painted their crafts."

"Sulfur - some sodium, oxygen and chlorine thrown into the mix. It's spewed out by the moon, and swept up into the magnetosphere of Jupiter. If the ship is breached, it will be everywhere." Delilah explained.

"What - it's a stinky salty rotten egg?" Boyd's grin could be heard through the static.

"Boyd - shut up!" Adair snapped with more frustration in his voice then he would have preferred come out.

Delilah ignored both of them continuing her scans. She started reading aloud, with the ships recorder also logging the information. "Main power is offline - auxiliary power is active. That means life-support will still be operational. The Pioneer has extensive damage to its port engine nacelle - there is evidence of coolant venting on the hull. The ship is drifting with a 2 degree per second 27 degree yaw lateral roll. The underside is coming into view - extensive hanger damage. Lower decks have breaches - there is no debris field probably due to the charged particle blowing it away."

"How do you know all that stuff, D? You're just making that shit up to sound all smart." Boyd quips, his landing craft pulling into the lead as it slowly matched the rotation and then edges into the shredded remains of the landing bay.

"Because I pay attention - you lout." Delilah answered back. "There isn't room for three ships in there - I'll stay out here and monitor."

"Check. I'm moving in." Adair acknowledged as his ship gingerly edged in to join Boyd's craft which had already landed and magnetically attached itself to the twisted deckplates.

-- == == --

The SS Beijing had begun to close on the alien contact. The returning strike-craft took a defensive triangular formation in front of the ship which allowed the Beijing to have line-of-sight targeting for it's X-ray lasers. A group of smaller sub-crafts broke away from the main target, and started to accelerate on a separate trajectory attempting to flank the defending craft and intercept the Pioneer. Responding to orders, the defending Sun-Tzu broke formation and shot forward to engage.

As the two primary craft drew closer, small explosions bubbled on the surface as X-ray lasers, unseen to the human eye impacted and blistered the skin of the Beijing before setting off small explosions inside.

-- == == --

The magnetic boots crunched onto the hull-plates of the landing bay of the USAS Pioneer sending up swirling eddies of yellowish-brown dust. Adair flanked by two marines joined up with Boyd and his guards in the landing bay.

"Looks like we missed the party here." Boyd glanced around the bay.

Delilah's voice was broken and staticy, and she was only meters away outside the twisted wreckage of the ship. "I can't… make you… interference."

Adair looked at Boyd, and then walked towards the opening. "We are seeing major damage to the landing bay. Extensive structural warping. No small crafts. We are experiencing severe radio interference. Suit-comp recorders are recording all data." He looked back, adding. "I'm not sure if she can read us. Let us continue inwards. Boyd - can you get through that door?"

Boyd walked over in microgravity to the unfamiliar hatch-way. It was rectangular with rounded corners and insets crossing for increased structural reinforcement. It was also bowed inward, and twisted by the impact which devastated the landing bay. The manual controls would be useless. "Looks like I need to use plan B." He pulled out a micro-torch from his utility belt. "Get ready for the hot-stuff"

"I think we're about to... hurry it up... going to get crowded." Adair heard Delilah crackle over the comms. He walked back to the gaping hole, but couldn't make out anything except the powerful vista - the other ships were simply too far to make out with the unaided eye.

"Hey - when you're done gawking - we're in." Boyd announced. His suit lights cut through the darkness inside, crisp unscattered beams. "The ship is depressurized. Hopefully the crew was able to get to vacc-suits."

"I think they have!" Adair explains as he joins Boyd. From the darkness inside the hull dozens of suit lights lanced out, bright enough to cause the visor to darken to compensate. On an common radio band a query calls out. "Identify yourself."

Adair stepped forward. "I'm Lieutenant-Commander Adair Fox of the United World Space Force. We're the rescue party." A shudder rippled through the ship. "Enough of the chatty. Let's move."

Adair and the marines helped the remaining crew of the crippled Pioneer to the landing craft, helping the wounded who floated thanks to the microgravity and several stretches with patients wrapped in vacc-bubbles to keep them breathing.

"Hey Adair," Boyd quipped from across the bay. "I think this time you did it. And you didn't even have to blow anything up." His words are cut-off by a sudden bright white flash.

-- == == --

The dump shock of the simulation suddenly ending caused vertigo, a severe lancing pain through the cortex of all the cadets, and several seizures. The sudden signal spike ran the risk of causing permanent damage to their brains. As cadets cried out in pain and rolled off their tables, the normal subdued blue lighting of the Immersion Chamber was replaced with a red glow and an alert klaxon sounded.

10

Sun Tzu once wrote that there were 5 constant factors governing the art of war: Moral Law - that the people will follow their leaders and the choices they make; Heaven - or the environment of the battle; Earth - the distance and the battlefield; Commander - who is wise, courageous, strict and benevolent; and Method and Discipline - the means for which the army is commanded.

Sun Tzu went on to extol the science and virtues which were relied upon for centuries thereafter. Warfare was built on deception. Attacking when one seemed unable, and being near when the enemy suspects you are far.

The Hegemony held Humanity to rules and guidelines which they did not reveal, and acted as if these were absolutes. There were factions within the Hegemony which were far more deceptive.

These forces did not outright resist or protest the Hegemony and the control of the senior races - they would rather work inside the rules. Twisting and warping the interpretations and pushing races to commit actions which would ultimately end with them sabotaging their own efforts.

And those races would do whatever they could to avoid being exposed.

"Prelude to Hegemony"
Secretary-General Shelley Dione (ret.), UWSF - 2032

The D'rak N'li needed a calamity with the vague appearance of a natural disaster, but with control, precision and with the undeniably finality of intent. Type M-asteroids were a plentiful source of ammunition, but unaugmented they would not suffice. Quickly enhanced by fusing the outer-shell of the asteroids until they were harder than metal, the asteroids were then accelerated at carefully guided trajectories to bring them all into Earth's orbit. The asteroids were carefully chosen to be below the threshold of size detectable by Earth until it was too late to react. The high metallic content allowed the D'rak N'li to use linear accelerators to quickly target a large number of these at the planet. There would be no evidence left at the impact sites, and the D'rak N'li would be gone long before the Mara would expand their plodding search to the asteroid belt.

Alien AI intelligences guided the final aiming to a 100 meter accuracy, taking into account the millions of kilometers and the turbulent interference caused by the Earth atmosphere upon reentry.

The D'rak N'li fleet worked for several days until a veritable swarm of dense metallic-core fused shelled asteroids were poised to rain down upon the Earth.

When initially detected, the researchers initially discounted the blips as noise or errors in the system. No objects should be travelling that quickly on perfect trajectories towards Earth. Double and triple checking revealed the news with only five hours advance notice.

The world governments moved to protect their leaders, however there simply was no time to prepare, or even notify the general populus.

The first hardened asteroid impacted China, aimed at the industrial boroughs of Shanghai. Factories which produced parts and components for the Chinese space fleet were obliterated on contact. A six kilometer long, 1 kilometer deep crater is left. Most of Shanghai suffers extreme devastation from the impact, fireball, and then earthquake caused by the impact.

The next asteroid impacts the Pacific Ocean. The floor of the ocean is cratered, and tsunamis are sent against the Japanese and Chinese coasts. The world starts to reel as the devastation in the East mounts. Astronomers start to search for an errant meteor which had broken up to cause the simultaneous impacts.

Two more impacts land in the Pacific Ocean as the world government tries to coordinate their immediate actions. The tsunamis advancing towards the west coast of the United States does not beat the next asteroid.

Los Angeles and Seattle are almost simultaneously struck. The loss of life and damage is catastrophic as the military and technical infrastructure is attacked. Mojave, Houston, New York, Miami, Chicago, Toronto, Asteroids batter North America leaving millions dead instantly and tens of millions injured, displaced or lost. The survivors have to contend with tsunamis and earthquake aftershocks as the asteroids then impact the Atlantic Ocean.

By this point the world is being shaken by the repeated impact of the meteors. Every impact leaves kilometer long craters killing millions and disrupting infrastructure. World resources start to mobilize to save the injured and try to contain the damage to the affected regions.

Europe is the last to be hit - although there is no protection from the mass panic. Millions try to flee the major cities, but cannot escape far enough as the major economic and military centers are hit with pin-point accuracy. London, Paris, Madrid, Berlin, Geneva, … the list continued as every major manufacturing, military or infrastructure target were peppered with reinforced asteroids.

-- == == --

Adair pushed himself up, feeling the twang of pain down his side. Dust was falling from the ceiling streaming through the red glow of the emergency lights. The floor was also moving, shaking unnaturally. Adair's first thought was to suspect it might be an earthquake. Never having experienced one before, he had nothing else to compare it against.

"Oh… man. That sucked." Boyd's voice came from the bed adjacent to Adair's.

"And here, I got to be the hero that time." Boyd called over to Adair from Delilah's side. "What do you think is going on? Why is the floor shaking?"

One of the light fixtures shook itself loose, falling down to clatter on the floor. Adair forced himself up and stumbled over to Boyd's bed. "Earthquake?" He shared his thought. "We need to make sure everyone is safe."

Boyd pulled himself out of the bed, the adrenaline of the moment overcoming his usual sim-exhaustion, and then went to check on Delilah while Adair went to Alphosone's side.

"There is some sort of emergency going on." Adair explained, turning his attention to Alphosine as she returned to this consciousness. Around them other cadets were getting up and helping others up. The ground kept shaking, and two more lights fell from the ceiling down to the ground.

"We should get outside - it will be safer.

Alphosine first insisted that she and Adair help and check on her friends - Sophie was also in the simulation. Making their way across the room - her Immersion chair was empty. Alphosine looked around in growing fear, but Sophie was wrapped into a tight ball, hiding underneath the raised platform.

"Sophie - come on. It's time to go. Allons-y!" Alphosine and Adair helped Sophie up, supporting the blond as they regrouped with Boyd and Delilah.

"This doesn't feel like any regular earthquake. Back home I rode through the one that hit back in '28, and it felt different." Boyd pointed out. The group started to make their way around the offline Immersion beds and towards the exit.

"Watch out." Boyd shouted as he used his bulk to shove the entire group aside as a light fixture crashed down where they were standing.

"Thanks big Johnson." Delilah says, holding onto Boyd's side. "Let's get out of here." She then looked over to Alphosine and said with playfulness "Allons-y indeed! Maybe now we can real action."

Adair looked back at Delilah with a bizarre expression on his face. "I think you've been hanging around Boyd too much." and then looked at Boyd. "And this certainly isn't a game."

The group of five helped other cadets groggy from the sudden drop of the simulation on their way to the exit before spilling out into the hallway. Strange unnatural shadows were cast, and there were spider-web like cracks on several of the external-facing windows.

Adair pulled the group to the side. He accesses one of the wall computer panels.

"Elisha - report."

The display panel replaced the 'EVACUATION WARNING' message with a map of the school. About half of the buildings flash in red indicating a life-threatening situation and evacuation zones were marked.

"There is an unknown emergency going on. I suspect that there has been an earthquake causing minor damage throughout the complex. MESH contact has been interrupted - I am attempting to restore MESH contact outside this complex. Please do not panic - this earthquake registers 5.8 on the Richter scale and does not pose a threat to this complex."

"I am telling you. This isn't a normal earthquake. It feels wrong." Boyd protests

Sophie spoke at last, pulling Alphosine towards the window. "Regardez!"

The group moved over to the window, looking northward. The clouds had an unnatural red glow from beyond the horizon. The clouds also had the appearance of swiss cheese, with several expanding holes like ripples in a pond. Fragments split from the primary asteroid continued to rain down, leaving bright red tracers in the distant sky.

"That's in the direction of Milan." Delilah commented.

The sky started to darken, and a greyish ash started to fall from the skies like an unnatural infernal snow - on winds blowing from the north and not from the oceans to the south as usual.

"This isn't an earthquake." Adair echoed Boyd's comment. "Something big hit north of here." Adair's face showed his distraction. This was too convenient. The odds of a meteor impact of this magnitude so close to the base must have been astronomical. Why was there no warnings? Why was there no evacuation? Cadets pushed by them in the hall, first in a panic to run outside, then in a panic to get back in as the ejecta started to fall.

Alphosine looked at the grey ash which had started collecting in the cracks in the glass and on the branches of the trees outside. "I don't understand. How big? Where?"

Adair went back to the computer panel. "Elisha - calculate the effects. The largest meteorite which could be not detectable by Earth orbital telescopes -

hitting Milan with enough force to cause the earthquake we are experiencing." As Elisha started to work, he turned back to address the group. "I don't think this is an accident."

"I'm sorry Adair - The maximum size for an orbital body to create this level of devastation does not have the velocity nor the density to cause this level of damage. The orbital body would need to be larger - at which point we would have had early detection, or be made from unknown materials and be going at a velocity to allow it to strike the Earth before being broken apart by atmospheric reentry."

Alphosine came to his elbow. "Aliens - Adair what if you are right?" She looked slightly fearful at the computer.

Delilah came close, and Adair and Alphosine gave her space. Delilah frowned at the computer panel, regarding it with distrust. Elisha knew something, and she was going to get it out of the computer. "What if it was artificially shot from the asteroid belt - they took heavy-metal asteroids, did some alien alchemy to turn them into mass-driver gauss bullets, and shot them at the Earth. Calculate what would be required to create a meteor impact of this magnitude."

There was a slight pause before Elisha responded with her calculations on the screen, "The maximum orbital velocity is 72.8 kilometers per second. If the nickel-iron core of a 120 meter asteroid was compressed to twice the standard density of an asteroid, then it would be causing an effect which is mathematically similar to what we are experiencing."

Delilah and Adair stepped back - stunned.

"What would happen to the impact site?" Sophie said with a mousy voice.

"The simulated impact site would be vapourized. There would be a seven kilometer crater and total destruction within a hundred kilometers." Elisha replied deadpan. It showed a simulation of the seven kilometer long crater overlaid over a map of Milan. "The ejecta cloud and earth quake would be similar to what we are experiencing."

Adair turned to Delilah. "They missed us. Unless they intended to hit Milan. Unless this isn't the only impact." He turned back to the computer, "Elisha - I know the MESH is disrupted. Run a query - which major centers have no MESH contact."

There is another pause - a loud crack startled the group as one of the upper windows suddenly cracked along it's entire length. The shaking of the ground had started to subside.

"In the last 8 hours, MESH contact has been lost with Shanghai, Tokyo, Los Angelos, Seattle, Houston, Mojave, Miami, New York…" Elisha started to drone on, to be cut off by Delilah

"Major world centers - going west to east." Delilah gripped Adair's shoulder, her eyes panic. "That's hundreds of millions of people - and they will think it's just an accident."

Sophie gasped as the list of cities included Paris before Delilah interrupted. Alphosine left Adair's arm to comfort Sophie.

"Isn't it?" Boyd joined in. "You know..million to one? An asteroid breaking up or something?"

"No Boyd. We would have detected anything that would have caused this level of devastation. That thing on the moon - they have got to be behind this." Delilah tried to explain.

Boyd looked back at Delilah, "Thing on the moon? You crashed on the moon. I think your head needs to be checked, D." he looks over at Adair who was sharing a look with Delilah "What… you too? Adair - this isn't some big alien conspiracy. It's just a tragedy."

"That's what it's meant to look like." Adair returned to where Alphosine was quietly consoling Sophie, "We need to find someone we can trust." Taking Sophie's other side, him and Alphosine helped her up while Boyd and Delilah followed holding hands.

There was debris in the upstairs hallways, and fewer cadets around. The group was almost at the doors to the upper Immersion Chamber monitoring booth when Professor Sparling and Commandant Rees exited.

Adair gasped and waved to get their attention. The rest of the group stiffened at the senior officers.

"Sir. This isn't an accident. I suspect that Earth is under attack - the fleet will be vulnerable as well. And our colonies."

"Cadet Fox. There is an emergency situation going on. Now is not the time for your alien ramblings." The Commandant did not trust the aliens, but such an open attack seemed so out of place. His military training told him to deal with the natural disaster and wait for orders - not to go chasing boogey-men in the night.

"It's true. Delilah - tell him what Elisha calculated." Adair stepped aside, knowing that Delilah could explain it better.

"The details of the meteor strikes, Sir. They couldn't happen in nature. It's not just here either - It is happening all over the world. They are coming too fast, and are too precisely targeted hitting major centers moving eastward as the planet rotates. Hell, sir - we couldn't pull off a shot like that if we tried."

"A shot like what, cadet?" Professor Sparling stepped forward to regard Delilah and Adair.

"They must be launched from the asteroid belt - that's where there are plentiful minerals." Explained Delilah. "The asteroids chosen to be under human detection size. And they have been augmented - like a depleted uranium round - to be harder than any common mineral. They are also accelerated to hit Earth - and have been precisely hitting major cities across the globe."

Another shockwave hit the building - this was a harder impact - the lights flickered and then went out and several of Elisha's panels shot sparks across the room. The groaning sound of metal slowly fatiguing and bending could be heard above them.

"You have no proof. You have hunches and are obviously biased based on ... " the Commandant paused "the recent experiences. We need to first see to the safety of everyone on this base, and then wait for orders."

Debris fell down around them. The building was slowly coming apart.

Adair stepped forward. "Sir, it's time to reveal everything to command in Geneva. They need to act. They need to know about the alien on the moon, about the simulation, about the Mara coverup."

There was a sudden groaning overhead as one of the major wall struts groaned and gave way. Professor Sparling turned, pushing the Commandant out of the way as lighting and hvac fixtures fell onto the catwalk between where they were standing.

"We need to have communications - to know what's going on. Sparling! You'll go with them." Commandant Rees coughed as he regained his footing amidst the debris before continuing. "Cadet Adair Fox. I'm hereby giving you a promotion to the rank of Lieutenant. Cadets Telford; Cadet Johnson; Cadet Fuluhea and Cadet Sinclair - you are all promoted to the rank of Lieutenant. You need to take your evidence to the United World Space Force command in Geneva. You will also relay our current situation and request a UWSF Liaison Team until formal communications can be re-established "

More debris fell down around them, dusting their shoulders. "GO!" commanded the base commander in an authoritarian voice.

The group turned and ran back towards the staircase going down. The lower hallways were devoid of cadets. The ground shifted with further aftershocks, sending the cadets sprawling to the floor.

Professor Sparling looked back up the stairs at the commander at the top, "What about you, Sir?"

"I need to stay here and look after the school. Take care of the kids." Instead of heading outside, the commandant ran deeper into the corridor connecting the N-E-P building with the Administration complex.

The group turned and pushed a cracked door open to enter one of the court-yards. There was now a thin layer of greyish soot covering the ground. The tall smoked windows of the two story N-E-P building was cracked in many places sending spider-web like branches reaching upwards. The sky was an unnatural reddish-brown colour with heavy low black clouds - a dingy smog of the airborne particles were being lit from below from the impacts. There was a breeze blowing from the north - not off the ocean as usual, a faint rumbling like a far off thunder-storm and the smell like of broken stone in the air.

"I need to get some things." Delilah pulled the group to a stop. She reached up to brush soot from her eyelashes. "Don't worry, I'll be back" She called out as she turned and changed course to run towards the Quads.

"You need to hurry - and to be safe." Adair looked at her. Boyd reached out towards Delilah, but she was already out of even his impressive reach. Her eyes sought out his and she mouthed 'be strong' before turning and covering her face from the hot stinging ash filling the air.

Adair ignored the exchange between Boyd and Delilah, instead turning to the professor. "I think we may need some supplies - there may be wounded there." His eyes showed that his concerns ran deeper - Adair wanted to play it safe.

Sparling nodded. "I agree. Johnson - you're with me. Let's get us something to keep us all safe." The professor reached over to clap the large black man on the shoulder.

Boyd cracked a wide grin and gave a playful marine grunt of agreement, "Oorah!"

The large black man and the shorter teacher ran off in direction of the academy armory.

"We should stay and help with the survivors." Alphosine suggested. There was a firm determination in her voice - she knew about these aliens and was eager to do what she could to help the base. Sophie clung to her friend's arm and nodded her agreement.

Adair turned to face her. "Al - I'm going to need you. We're going to Geneva, and the computers may be out. You're the best linguistI know - and you speak French, German, English and lord knows what else, and all without needing translators. I think you would be really valuable to help in Geneva" He turns to Sophie. "You could stay and organize the cadets. Once the base is taken care of, you could send a team north to assist. Remember, Lieutenant - it's up to us to show leadership and calm."

Sophie nodded, standing up and releasing Alphosine's arm. She smiled and gained some courage from Adair's comments. "I could do that." she said hesitantly, and then looked back to Alphosine for some guidance.

Alphosine spoke to her in French, with slow understanding tones. "Go and get two people to help you out. They can help you organize the rest. Organize teams to search and rescue anyone hurt from the buildings. Get some of those tents from the Commissary and set up a medical facility. You will also need to get kitchen set up. You don't need to do it alone - get others to help. Be a leader for them." She gave Sophie a kiss on the cheek. "Allons-y"

Sophie turned to run towards the Quads, leaving Adair and Alphosine alone.

"I'll go with you." Alphosine agreed turning back towards Adair, her voice seeming so out of place amidst the ashen debris blowing around them.

Adair paused and timidly took Alphosine's hands, looking her deep into her light brown eyes. "It seems like we're always running someplace, or someone is interrupting. We don't have time to... talk."

Alphosine blushed slightly and gave Adair's hands a slight squeeze. Her eyes were unreadable, not giving any indication of her deeper thoughts. Adair just stared a moment longer, and then lead her across the campus.

The debris cloud was getting thicker, and it was getting difficult to breathe outside. Pausing under one of the awnings, and reaching to wipe the grime from their faces, Alphosine noted, "The ash is hot – it burns abit when it touches me."

"That makes sense – this is the fallout from the meteor." Adair coughed and spit out the dark grey mass. "I'm sorry to ask this, but can we..." Adair nodded towards the expensive scarf Alphosine wore around her neck.

Alphosine nodded and unwrapped the scarf, handing it to Adair.

"Sorry" Adair murmured, and then unwrapping the scarf, he tore it longitudinally in half, and doubling it up, and then reached to slowly fashion it into a covering to protect her face. Reaching around he gently tied it around her head. Alphosine took the other half, and leant forward to repeat the gesture, reaching her long slender arms in an almost embrace around Adair's head to tie the torn scarf around his face. Soon they were both wearing mirrored lavender silk masks over the lower half of their faces.

"Let's get going." Adair reached to hold both of Alphosine's arms for a moment, his fingers smearing the ash which had fallen onto her skin. He looked down at the constant reminder of the calamity before leading her back out into the falling debris.

The ground-port was covered by the same soot, intermixed with small rocks and bits of pulverized concrete. There were two Tsiolkovsky landing craft, a sleeker more aerodynamic American Huey-class landing craft (an American ship of the same type as the Tsiolkovsky-class), as well as 3 conventional helicopters. There were a number of cadets gathering at the gates, however the military police were restricting access.

Adair and Alphosine made their way through the crowd to the closed gate. Blocking the gate were a pair of military police dressed in full marine vacc-suits. With the dark grey soot gathering on their armour, they looked like some post-apocalyptic scavengers.

Adair managed to break through the front of the crowd, but before he could speak the MP held a hand before of Adair, "I'm sorry, cadets – the ground port is closed." There was an unhappy murmuring behind them from the gathered cadets.

"Sir – we are on a mission. We need to get to Geneva to notify command – Commandant Rees sent us." Adair replied. Nearby, cadets coughed as they huddled closer, listening in on the exchange.

"The MESH is down – we have no way to verify those instructions cadet. We need to secure the ground-port. It's very dangerous to fly in these conditions."

Adair realized that the MP were correct, and there wasn't any way he was about to bully himself past. "With the MESH down, there is no way you can receive any updated instructions. Besides, these people are in danger out here. They just want to take shelter inside the shuttles where they are protected from the falling debris." There was a murmuring of consent.

The guards were starting to reconsider when Adair kept pushing "Conventional aircraft can't work in this debris - but the spacecraft can. They are not air-breathing - and I have been sent by Commandant Rees to get to Geneva for further assistance and instruction."

The MPs reach up to resist Adair. "Just hold on a second!"

"He's telling the truth." A figure dressed in wilderness survival fatigues and wearing a balaclava pushed towards the front. "I have it on recording."

"I'm sorry, who are you?" The MP asked as the group parted to let the newcomer to the front.

"Lieutenant Delilah Telford." The newcomer explained mustering as much bravado and presence as she could muster. Lifting her personal wrist computer, she played back the conversation from earlier.

The playback was tiny-sounding coming from Delilah's personal recorder.

"Cadet Adair Fox. I'm hereby giving you a promotion to the rank of Lieutenant. Cadets Telford; Cadet Johnson; Cadet Fuluhea and Cadet Sinclair - you are all promoted to the rank of Lieutenant. You need to take your evidence to the United World Space Force command in Geneva. You will also relay our current situation and request a UWSF Liaison Team until formal communications can be re-established " There a rumble and a slight pause. "GO!"

The MP listened to the recording. "You could have faked that."

"Can you imagine the trouble we'd be in, if that was fake?" Delilah replied. "Impersonating an officer, stealing a landing craft, ..."

Adair touched Delilah's shoulder to restrain her complaints. "It's true. Look at what is going on. You're doing a good thing here, Warrant Officer, but we need to get to Geneva."

"It's too dangerous to fly." The MP offered a defense.

"The intake filters can handle it – and the landing craft are designed to work in a vacuum." Delilah shrugged off Adair's grip and spoke with a disdain for their ignorance.

The MP consider all of the evidence before agreeing. "Alright – you can pass." They moved to start unlocking and opening the gate.

"What about us... Bring us with you... Let us get at whoever caused this..." came the cries from behind.

Adair turned and addressed the crowd. "We are facing a crisis here. Not just here, but all over the world. Humanity has been attacked - each and every one of us has been targeted. We have been knocked to our knees. But we can pick ourselves up. We can stand together. We can WIN together!" The crowd, listening with rapt attention, gives out a cheer.

Adair pauses, looking over the gathered cadets, their faces blackened from the fallen ash, and continued. "I'm not going to sugar coat this to you. Tens of millions of died today. You might have lost someone you loved. Before we're done, more people will die. This is no simulation - this is no class or test. This is the survival of the human race!" The MPs joined in with the assembled cadets in cheering.

"What can we do?" called out someone from the back.

"There will be teams organized here to get anyone from the buildings. Go back to your quad and help organize those teams. Anyone here with technical abilities – these vehicles will be needed to ferry supplies and the injured. This" he reached upwards to catch some soot. "Will not hold us back – but you will be needed to maintain what we have, and fix those are broken. Help each other. All of our hands are needed now."

A roar of applause and cheer spread through the cadets. Adair, Delilah stepped forward to present themselves to the crowd. When they turned, the MP at the gate were also saluting him. They walked to the open gate.

"Professor Sparling and Boyd Johnson will be joining us shortly. Send them over - we need to get the craft prepped for take off. And don't waste your time guarding a gate - HELP OUT! People need to be rescued!" Adair turned to the rest of the crowd. "If there are any technicians who can get the rest of the craft working, please come forward. We will all need all the resources we can muster."

Adair, Delilah and Alphosine entered the ground station, and choosing the closest Tsiolkovsky, headed over. It was one of the landing craft assigned to the base itself - the UWSF Hoja Caída - SV/TL-124.

"That sounds good, but what are your grandiose plans. You make it sound like you're going to lead the charge yourself." Alphosine said quietly.

Adair is about to answer when Delilah pulled both him and Alphosine towards the ship.

"Don't you know, honey - Adair is all speeches. And I'm glad I got that one - you had them all going." Delilah agreed. "Now, I'll start pre-flight but can you two can climb up there and clean as much of the soot off the HEPE and intakes?" She released them and cycled the airlock.

Adair nodded, and nodded to Alphosine, leading her to the side of the craft. "Be careful Al"

Adair first helped Alphosine up the stubby wing before climbing up the opposite side of the craft. Both used their hands to clear the vents. Nearby other cadets started to work on making the other vehicles operational.

Boyd and Sparling approached, both wearing heavy all-weather fatigues, helmets and with slung gauss carbines. Each of them also had a heavy duffel-bag slung over their other shoulder.

"This is impressive, Lieutenant Fox." Sparling commented, noting to how the unruly mob of cadets had been dispersed, and instead the cadets and MP were working together. He ducked down and entered the landing craft.

Boyd paused outside the ship. He looked up at Adair and grinned. "Looks like I get to save you again, Fox. And save the world." He looked up at Adair and Alphosine with a teasing smirk. "Twice in one day - I don't know where you'd be without me, Fox."

With a wide grin, Boyd ducked into the landing craft. His jocular tone could be heard through the open hatch.

Adair finished clearing the soot from the intakes, glanced over to get a thumbs up from Alphosine, and then reaches down to bang on the hull. As he climbs down he hears hears the engines humming to life. Alphosine holds the hatch open for him, closing it behind as Adair makes his way towards the cockpit. On the way, he passes Boyd and Sparling who have stowed the gear and are strapped in to the seats nearest to to the door.

The hatch to the cockpit is open, and the Delilah is strapped into her seats finishing the pre-flight preparations. Alphosine wiggles past him and takes the co-pilot seat and starts working on the comm's controls.

"Take us out, as quick as we can." Adair says to Delilah. "As soon as we're ready."

The SS Hoja Caída lifted off from the pad and climbed into the air. It quickly rose through the thickest part of the soot and climbed into the ashen sky - when it was a safe distance from the people on the ground Delilah activated the main Plasmics on higher thrust to guide the ship to a wide suborbital parabolic towards Switzerland.

Adair stood in the hatch with hands on the back of both command chairs, watching the blue skies as the craft finally pierced the sooty veil settling around southern Spain. A soft sob brought his attention to Alphosine. He looked at her to see tears streaming down her face.

"Tellement de personnes train de mourir." She whispered under her breath.

Adair moved to hold her shoulders. "Al - what are you hearing?" he asked softly.

She reached up to wipe tears, composing herself.

"Nombreuses personnes… There are so many people dying. It is charivari out there. Everybody is talking at once."

Adair squeezed her shoulder. "We need to talk to command - someone in charge."

As the Hoja Caída lifted higher and higher on a plume of super-heated plasma, Spain shrunk and more of Europe was visible. Through the clouds and dust an ugly crater could be seen where Madrid was. It was not alone.

Bonn laid obfuscated by a black cloud – under lit by fires. London showed another crater - with a second one on the British Isles in the north - the location of the UWSF shipyards in Scotland. As the landing craft climbed higher and higher, more and more of the destruction could be seen. The surface of the planet was scarred and the clouds showing the wounds of the impacts.

-- == == --

As the ship reached apogee, Boyd and Professor Sparling pushed to either side of Adair to look out the cockpit windows. Everyone stared in rapt horror at the planet below.

Dozens of impact craters gave the Earth a slight swiss-cheese look. Black clouds were competing with the white ones to cover the face of the planet with a bruised stain. The silent Earth below continued in it's path as the humans on the surface dealt with the world-shattering tragedy.

"Go back." Adair said softly.

"But, Geneva?" asked Delilah.

"Its gone. Turn back." Adairs voice was deflated. He knew that the world had been hit, but they were just words before. Now looking down at the devastation it had started to really sink in the extent of the damage. "There won't be anyone left there to report to. We are on our own."

Alphosine suddenly sat up. She adjusted some controls, and then spoke into the headset.

"Bùmíng shēnfèn de chuánzhī, qǐng shìbié nǐ zìjǐ."

Adair turned and looked. "I didn't know you spoke Chinese."

"Mandarin." Alphosine corrected. "Its a ship. The... umm... the Pānyú. It was going to Paris when the attack came. They can't reach the Imperial High Command."

"I'd expect not. These attacks are precise and took out all of Earth's major command and infrastructure." An idea started to occur. "See if they are willing to join us. Send them the coordinates to come back to the academy."

Alphosine started to work. Adair paused to admire her hair - even with the flakes of ash in it, she looked almost angelic sitting over the comms, her soothing voice speaking chinese as she provided directions to the other ship. Adair sighed softly before ducking back into the rear of the ship to brief Boyd and Sparling.

When he returned, Alphosine was still hard at work, speaking in several languages to all the other comm-receivers within their range. The MESH may be down, but they could still reach out to those within the range of their landing craft - which was pretty extensive.

"We have three more shuttles coming, two American strike craft from France, and the Chinese cutter. What are you thinking?"

Adair turned to Delilah. "They hit all of the ground targets. But there are bound to be ships in orbit... or those at the orbital proving grounds. What can you find out?"

Delilah turned to the computer. The public MESH serving the populace was not fragmented and not operational, however through Telford Industries Delilah was able to access the private Military-Industrial Complex MESH. She ran several queries and studied the holo readouts.

Delilah spoke over her shoulder. "There are some proving grounds... but they won't have a crew."

"Good thing I know where there are plenty of trained people." Adair beamed. "Take us back to the academy. I need to speak to Admiral Rees."

-- == == --

The approach to the academy showed the damage even four hundred kilometers from the blast center. Glass was broken or shattered, several buildings had partially collapsed and black soot choked the trees. But there were hopeful signs too. The ground-port had been cleared of debris and was being used to stage supplies going out to nearby towns. Two large white medical tents were set up and surrounding that was a growing city of military survival tents. The base had opened up and were taking in nearby displaced civilians.

The incoming ship was not alone. It lead a flight now of eight helicopters, two light civilian planes, four Tsiolkovsky landing craft, two UWSF Sun-Tzu strike craft from Italy, three American Eagle strike craft and an American Huey landing craft, and the Pānyú - large (compared with the shuttles) Chinese cutter. The cutter was forced to fly south to land in the ocean - there was no landing surface nearby large or reinforced enough to take the weight. A flight of pontoon helicopters departed to bring the Chinese back. The Hoja Caída landed at the academy. Ground- teams came out to start tendering the craft.

"I'm going to find the Admiral. Boyd... we are going to need some troops. When we find them, we will need to teach these guys a lesson. Delilah, we're going to need technicians and infrastructure - especially if we are now also interfacing with civilian, American and Chinese ships." Boyd and Delilah nodded consent and ran off.

"Alphosone... Find Sophie and her team. We are going to need to get some crew together. Also, when the Pānyú arrive, I don't think many will be able to talk to them. They will be cut-off, alone and scared."

"I'm scared too, Adair." she answered softly, pausing to look up at him, drawing courage from him. "I'll round up the communication teams and make sure the Pānyú is taken care of."

"But you are not alone." He smiled at her. She nodded and then ran off. Adair watched her leave... it still wasn't the time nor place to tell her how he felt.

"Sir?" Adair turned to Professor Sparling.

"Soon, I'll be calling you Sir." the Professor had a proud look in his eyes. He knew he was right about Adair all along - he was the leader that Earth needed at a time like this. Compassionate, and responsible yet willing to take the initiative to obtain his goals.

"Can you come with me to find the Admiral? I could use your support."

"I'll come, but Adair - you don't need my support. You have this."

-- == == --

Partial power had been restored to the administration building. The wind turbine and solar panels were providing an alternate source to the bases damaged Eapo reactor. Inside was a mixture of military and civilians who were lending a hand - the Academy grounds transformed into a regional trauma and recovery centre. Adair was directed to a corner of the entrance hall which had been set up to allow civilian and military teams to coordinate the rescue and rebuilding efforts. Adair caught sight of Admiral Rees talking with a group of local civilian maintenance staff. Waiting for the Admiral to be finished. Adair sat down on an empty crate which was set off to the side and looked at his reflection in the cracked ash-covered glass. He was covered in grime, but had a steely determination in his eyes.

When he was finally available, Adair approached along with Professor Sparling.

"You are back early." Admiral Rees noted.

"We never got there, Sir. Geneva is just a crater. Same with near-system command in London and the shipyards in Scotland. It's not just us... every major military command has been hit." Adair paused. Taking a breath, he continued, "We managed to contact some other survivors. We brought back a couple Americans and even a Chinese cutter with us."

"Why did you do that?"

"To build up a fleet, Sir. All of our ground forces have been hit, but there will be ships at Gateway, at Independance. At Armstrong and Cyril ... at every major orbital and non-Earth base. There will be unmanned ships at the UWSF proving grounds... We are the only ones who know who is behind the attacks. We could probably pinpoint their location. All we need is an Admiral for the fleet."

Admiral Rees sat down and exhaled through his mouth. He withdrew a pipe, and while smoking was anachronistic and forbidden, he lit it and inhaled deeply. A long moment passed.

"If there was a command left... they might court martial me for this."

"Sir, I think we are what is left of command."

"I know, son. Let me think." He inhaled and blew out smoke. The old Commandant then reached over and pressed a button on the table.

"Midshipman, find me Commander Marshall and Lieutenant Commander Vickers. Send them in immediately. I also need to get a personal Yeoman - someone who isn't flighty." he paused and looked up at Adair and Sparling.

"Start making arrangements. We need to get any able crew prepared and any orbital landing craft and strike craft ready to depart for Gateway. Send a ship to Independence and Project 10-something..whatever that blasted Chinese station was called. Sparling, keep our boy out of trouble."

Sparling saluted. "Yes Sir!"

"Dismissed."

-- == == --

Adair caught up with Delilah outside the cadet dorms where she was reviewing the records she has managed to piece together using her personal computer. While the public MESH was down, Delilah was able to correlate what little data was available using her personal Telford credentials.

"Did you speak to Commandant Rees?" Delilah turned her attention to Adair.

"I did. We are starting to muster who we can. And also send landing crafts to orbital bases which might have not been hit."

"Well, I have found something interesting for you." She turned and called up some records.

A tiny holo of an Archimedes-class destroyer came up. It had similar lines to the normal ships, however its launch bay was stretched and enlarged to twice the size of a conventional Archimedes.

"What is that? It looks pregnant"

"Its a new variant Telford Industries was working on. It's a carrier variant - it holds ten strike craft rather than the normal three. It also has more torpedo tubes. Our simulations puts its combat effectiveness about par with a Galileo-class cruiser."

Adair whistled in appreciation. "What are the drawbacks?"

"It isn't as aerodynamic as a regular Archimedes-class. They aren't equipped with landing gear - nor do they have the full operational range. They were designed more for system defense."

"Where is it?" Adair looked on with interest.

"The Telford Proving Grounds - based out of the Lagrange point. But it won't have any crew, or any armaments or strike craft."

Adair reached to put a hand on Delilah's shoulder. "Delilah - that was amazing. When you have the details set, go to the ground port. I'll meet you there - with our crew."

Sparling had been standing there listening the entire time. "I'll go and get us a landing craft prepped, Lieutenant." He paused to salute Adair, and receiving a salute back, left for the ground port.

"He said one day he'd salute me." Adair commented after his former professor departed. He turned and headed into the temporary tent-city.

-- == == --

Adair found Alphosine with Sophie and some other cadets setting up administration and logistics for the influx of people. They were busy talking with people coming in, switching between Spanish and French as they registered refugees and dealt with base personnel and civilian workers alike.

"Hi Al, Hi Sophie" Adair smiled.

Sophie seemed to have changed - she was devoted to organizing the people and managing the logistics of the displaced cadets and civilians. Somewhere along the way she had managed to clean up, although her uniform was still streaked with the ash which was everywhere.

Alphosine smiled as Adair approached and greeted them. "Did you talk to the Commandant?"

"Yes I did. Delilah has found us a ship, but we're going to need to find some crew. And some of the other ships joining us will require crew too."

"I'm sure I can find people who are eager to get out of here and strike back at whoever did this." Sophie volunteered.

Alphosine nodded and smiled. "I can help you Sophie. We will get the crew for you, Adair. You could take time to clean up and get a fresh uniform." Alphosine offered at the end.

Adair blushed and nodded. "What about the Chinese?"

Alphosine nodded towards an area where several officers in light tan uniforms with blazing red People's Republic of China logo were helping to set up and distribute food and sundry supplies.

Adair watched the Chinese soldiers working side by side with those from the United World Space Force. "We will want them to come along. We're assembling a fleet at Gateway Station."

Alphosine nodded. "I will tell them. We will get all of the available cadets and staff for crewing the ships too, but I am only coming if you go and clean up." she adds with a sweet teasing smile.

"I'm going, I'm going." Adair resisted reaching out to her in his current start. He headed back towards his quad.

-- == == --

The exterior wall of glass for his dorm had shattered, probably ruining what clothing he had left, so Adair detoured to a makeshift commissary to get an officer functional uniform complete with Lieutenant pips before retiring to his room.

The communal showers were working, and after cleaning up, he carefully picked through the broken glass to look at his room. Three of the walls still in place were cracked but still attempted to display snow-ladened trees and an ice-covered pond. The images flickered and shifted out of phase sporadically.

Adair righted his chair, and sat. The computer desk showed a litany of error messages. Adair reached to disable them, but his control surface was broken and glitching. Suddenly the screen cleared and reformed in the image of a Mara. The head-crest of the Mara was tall, and slightly more ornate than the average Mara.

"Greetings Agriprom Prime Lalrit. As you can imagine, we are rather busy. Can I help you?" Adair did little to hide his attitude towards the Mara; his tone was curt.

"A great tragedy has occurred. The Hegemony is most apologetic."

"However you cannot interfere... yadda yadda. Listen, Agriprom Prime. I don't have time for apologies, only for solutions. And since your kind isn't offering any of those, I don't have time for you. " Adair snarked back at the holo.

The Mara cut Adair off, his tone firmer than any he had heard before from a Mara."These are Hegemony issues which we are investigating. You would be advised to not involve yourself in matters that you do not understand."

Adair stood up, putting his hands down to look at the table fiercely. "Not understand? MILLIONS of humans are dead. MILLIONS! As far as I'm concerned, you Mara might has well pulled the trigger yourself. If you get in the way of us protecting Earth, you will pay the price."

"Are you threatening me, Lieutenant Adair Fox?" Lalrit's tone had returned to it's careful neutrality.

"I'm explaining the situation. I don't have any more time to waste with you." Unable to cut the signal, Adair stood and stalked towards the exit. He paused and looked back at the holo "You Mara could have at least pretended to be concerned about the millions who had perished."

Agriprom Prime Lalrit regarded Adair's departure impassively as he stalked out of the destroyed room for a moment, before the screen went blank.

-- == == --

"Where have you been?" Delilah asked as Adair approached.

As Adair was about to answer Alphosine interjected, "You look much better." She smiled at Adair before returning to coordinate logistics with the chinese officers.

"Thank you." Adair smiled back at Alphosine, before continuing, "I had a little chat with a Mara. They expressed their condolences and told us to stay out of their investigation."

"Oh... thats rich!" Delilah snapped shortly. "Sorry for our alien friends killing millions, but keep your nose out."

"More or less. We ready?"

Delilah nodded and grinned. "As Alphosine would say, Allons-y."

The landing craft lifted into the air, and turned towards the sky. Around them, other ships also lifted off. To the south, the large bulbous Chinese cutter joined the small flotilla climbing into the sky. Most of the smaller craft were UWSF craft however a couple foreign military craft and a few corporate shuttles joined the mix.

As they climbed higher Alphosine turned and commented "Our FleetMESH is expanding - more ships are joining us as we go up. The WorldMESH is starting to re-establish itself."

"Can you get a message to the Admiral's craft. Notify him that we will rejoin the fleet at Gateway Station. And then get a message to some of our academy shuttles - give them the Telford Proving Grounds approach codes and have them follow us in."

Adair touched Alphosine's shoulder. "Affirmative." She replied.

"Take us to that orbital facility. Can you relay the access codes to the rest of our little fleet - so that we can crew the ship."

Delilah turned around and looked at Adair. "You are serious about this. This isn't some sim, you know. This is real. And these are real aliens we are going up against. Not to mention you could very well call this Grand-Theft-Spaceship... it's not like command gave you a sudden promotion to Captain Buck Rogers"

"I am serious. No one else knows what we do. And no other human have met these aliens.

Admiral Rees trusts in us. And we won't be forcing anyone to come."

"I just hope that still sounds good at your court martial" retorted Delilah. "If there are enough pieces left to court martial, that is." She tapped the commands on her wrist to transfer the control codes to Alphosine.

-- == == --

As the cluster of ships approached the Telford Orbital Testing Station at the L2 Lagrange point, automated satellites tracked and queried the fleet. Giving the passcodes, and with a lack of responses from the ground-based facilities, the satellites choose to accept and admit the ships.

The testing ground had minor orbital facilities, but was not designed for constant ongoing habitation, but rather to be used while a ship is undergoing review. There was an enclosed spacedock large enough to fit a Galileo class cruiser, with several docking ports for tsiolkovsky landing craft around the edges. Currently there was a civilian SpaceShipFour class orbital shuttle docked.

Inside the cage-like spacedock rested the pregnant looking Archimedes destroyer. Along the side of the ship was the name UWSS Canary Island - SS/Dc-01. The ship looked brand new, and several of the access ports were still covered with bright orange construction coverings. Several long umbilicals connected the ship to the surrounding cage. Around the outside of the spacedock protruded several trusses which contained old-style solar panels. On one side was a long cone-like EM catcher module designed for capturing cargo modules slung from the lunar surface.

Cycling the docking hatch, Adair floated out through the flexible skinned access tube and through another hatch into the EVA module of the station. Three technicians wearing orange and yellow jumpsuits were waiting.

"Military? Lieutenant, we were expecting a ship from the company. You were using company credentials when you approached." Adair opens his mouth to reply, when suddenly the three looked past him.

Delilah floated through the airlock, and nodded towards the technicians.

"You're Delilah Telford?" one asked as the attention turned to her. "What happened – we were watching the Earth as all of the meteors hit. It was like World War III down there."

The rest of the cadets started to float into the EVA module.

"You described it well. Earth is under attack." Adair floated back towards the front.

"We are amassing a fleet of what ships are able at Gateway Station."

The technicians looked back and forth.

"The Canary Island isn't flight worthy. It's not finished all of the flight checks, it hasn't been loaded with armaments – and there aren't any crafts loaded. Plus we aren't authorized to release the ship."

Delilah and Adair floated close. "Don't you understand? There isn't anyone left to release it. It will take months for command to re-establish itself. Even longer for things to return to normal. We need to save Earth – to make sure that there /will/ be a command left." Adair regarded them steely.

"We're going to need your help – no one knows the Canary Island as good as you do. We'll need you on-board the ship." Delilah continued.

The technicians looked at the cadets who were gathering in the bay. They looked back and forth, and then nodded.

"Who's in charge?"

-- == == --

Adair settled into the command chair. Around the bridge Delilah, Alphosine, and other cadets were busy taking plastic protective seals off of the consoles. Several of the computer panels were not completely installed, and everything had that 'new' feel to it.

Behind him on one of the engineering consoles, one of the technicians named Fredrico Angelos was running the ship through its power-up routines. Everyone was working, with the exception of Adair. He knew not to disturb people and let them go through their routines.

Looking down at the various holo-controls at his fingertips, he called up the internal monitors and called up the landing bay on the main screen. The Canary Island logo derezzed and displayed a high view of the large chamber. Instead of the proper compliment of strike craft, the bay was mostly filled with Tsiolkovsky landing craft and the SpaceShipFour shuttle. The crew were busy stowing the craft and preparing the landing bay for actual flight.

"Sir, I'm sorry but there are no armaments on base." Fredrico commented out of the blue.

"I'm hoping we will be able to get some armaments at Gateway. Or possibly at Independence or at Ten-Twelve."

"I don't think the Americans or the Chinese would be willing to share with us." The technician doubted.

"You'll see Fredrico. It's a new world, and we all have a much bigger threat now."

Adair released the visual, and waited as the various departments started giving their greens. Checklists were completed, the engines were primed and the SS Canary Island was ready to go.

-- == == --

"Would you look at that sir? It's like a party there. I don't think there have ever been so many ships in one place in... well... ever."

The viewscreen showed the United World Gateway Station, even incomplete it was the largest human space-station. Only Armstrong Base on the Moon and Cyril and Giovanni bases on Mars were bigger off-Earth settlements. And yet, every orbital docking was taken up, and arrayed around the base in low-perturbation orbits were ships of several countries. The fleet was not just small ships, either.

The flagship was the UWSS Hermes - the Galileo class cruiser where Admiral Rees had taken his command. It lead the SS Canary Island, along with the SS Madrid and SS Brasilia, both the new Avia variants of the Archimedes, and the SS Bonn, SS Paris and SS Beijing.

From the American fleets Admiral Mordecai Balaban was on the USAS Devon Wolfe (Named after the 59th President of the United States) The American Flag ship was accompanied by two Destroyers (USAS Nevada and USAS New York) and a small group of cutters: USAS Voyager, USAS Cassini, USAS Pioneer and USAS Dynasoar. There were also a pair of military freighters designed for fleet support) - the USAS Lewis and Clark and USAS Wally Shirra.

Zhong jiang Wei-Ding Lei surprised everyone. The secret project (which most governments knew about, but the details were sketchy) was the Chinese cruiser which was launched only last year. Slightly late to the space race, the cruiser was meant to show Chinese supremacy. About 50% more massive than an American Thor class Cruiser, and sporting two long 'launching decks' the 837-Dalian bristled with weapons and had the capacity for fourteen Chengdu AAJ-5 combat crafts. It was accompanied by the 661-Beihai, a Chinese frigate and the 657-Panyu and 714-Shiyan both cutters.

There were also a small fleet of Civilian non-combatant ships. Both of the passenger variety, such as the Virgin Galactic SpaceShipFour and RpK Eurostar Sol tourist passenger ships, or the American Tarutius "Tar-Tar" and newer Gore class bulk freighters, to the Chevron Alaska Pride class build fluid transports originally designed to bring processed helium-3 back to the Earth system.

-- == == --

Adair found himself slightly overwhelmed as he floated through the access tubes from the weightless orbital bays. He was the same rank as the Lieutenant guiding him through the station towards the ward-room which had been converted into the central war-room for the upcoming campaign. Two other Captains were with him, having arrived at the same time - one of the civilian freighter captains wearing a leather jacket with patches sewn on it, and a severe looking Chinese captain.

The habitation modules of Gateway were under .6 G, enough to make walking possible and to give an 'up' and a 'down' sensation. The door cycled for the ward room, and the three arriving captains joined the group arrayed in the three rows of tables. Unconsciously, all of the different countries were tending to sit together. At the front of the room, Admiral Henry-Joseph Rees, Admiral Mordecai Balaban and Zhong jiang Wei-Ding Lei were talking quietly among themselves. Noting Adair's entrance, Admiral Rees motioned him over.

"Yes, Sir." Adair saluted as he bounded over in the light-gravity. The wizened Chinese Zhong jiang and rakish American Admiral looked at the young Lieutenant.

"This is Lieutenant Adair Fox - Captain of the Canary Island. He and one of his crew are the only two humans ever to have personally met the alien forces we anticipate we will be facing. As ease, Lieutenant. Do you have any personal insights you can share with us?"

Adair thought for a moment, replaying the scene on the lunar surface through his mind.

"They are cowardly - they attack when they cannot be seen, and have some sort of cloaking technology. But they also are sadistic - instead of outright killing their targets, they prefer to prolong the suffering as much as possible." Adair pauses. "This may have been the individual in question and may not be a racial trait. I've only met the one."

The Admiral presses a button and Adair's message is amplified to fill the room for the other captains.

"They use an invisible firing weapon that causes grievous damage to anything it hits. There is no known defence or protection from the weapon's effect. They also are technologically far advanced, and can tap and take over our computers. It is better to react to instinct than to trust your sensors."

"Physically they are not very impressive. They are shorter, with two pairs of arms and some type of membrane connecting, but that may have just been the design of their suit."

"Like the Mara - six limbs" one of the American captains noted.

"Like the Mara. They are fast, but their technology and reflexes can be defeated if they are focusing on one goal. In a straight one-on-one confrontation they have the far advantage. And it could be safe to assume they know we are coming."

"How do we know where they are? And that this just isn't a cosmic accident." One of the younger Chinese captains spoke up.

"The composition, speed and pin-point aim of the meteors allude to an intelligent directed sources. Plus these actions come 87 days after an incident on the lunar surface. Which is the time it would have taken the asteroids if launched from the Asteroid belt to reach Earth."

"How do you know where they are?"

This time Admiral Rees stepped forward. "We know where they were - the source of the meteors is fixed by the laws of physics. We will look for them there."

Admiral Balaban stepped up. "We have been given our fleet assignments. Because of the unique capabilities provided by our gathered forces, there will be some integration of the fleets under the respective Admirals. You will receive your assignments via FleetMESH. All captains will personally acknowledge and review the plans with your respective Admirals before leaving. Remember, we cannot trust technology."

Everyone turned towards the Chinese Zhong jiang. He said nothing.

"Dismissed. Report to your individual Admirals before leaving Gateway. Humanity is depending on us - all of us." Admiral Rees released the room.

Adair looked down to his personal computer, and was surprised by the marching orders. Along with the SS Bonn and SS Paris, his ship had been assigned to the fleet under Zhong jiang Wei-Ding Lei with the AS New York and the 657-Panyu and 714-Shiyan.

He reported to a smaller briefing room where the mixed group of captains had assembled. Zhong jiang Wei-Ding waited for the group to be settled before starting.

"We will be the tip of the spear - our fleet will be going in first to act as a lure for the enemies. We will have back-up, but we will be courageous and valiant. Many of you are young and inexperienced, and many of your crew will be looking up to you for guidance. You need to be strong and unwavering."

There was some murmuring, but no dissention. The captains knew they were looking to stop any future attacks on the Earth. The Zhong jiang finalized the logistical details of their mission.

11

There exists very little data on alien space craft - their capabilities, sizes or operational ranges. The only race we have had direct contact with are the Mara - and we have only seen the small landing craft they use for all system travel.

This is not so surprising, as we also have limited data on the ships which are flown by the Americans or Chinese. Specific operational parameters are kept as tight government secrets. While all ships use the similar core technologies - Eapo reactors, FT-Hop and HEPE Drives, AI Computers, and are all similarly armed with high-energy x-ray lasers, hyper-kinetic gauss cannons and self-guided torpedoes.

The smallest ships fielded by all armies are the Strike Craft - small one or two person ships designed specifically for ship-to-ship warfare. Landing Craft are used as personnel transport, and could be used for boarding actions.

While not fielded by the United World Space Force, both American and Chinese have small Cutter class. These crafts are highly aerodynamic and used as large landing crafts or capital ship support.

The current main-stay of most space-navys are the Destroyer class of ships. Fielded by all major fleets, the UWSF Archimedes comes in three variations each designed for special mission profiles. The base model is supported by an extended range exploration, while the combat capacities was extended by the carrier model.

American and United World both field a cruiser class - larger capital ships designed to be the future main-stay of the fleets.

The Chinese had started to fall behind, resulting in a fresh push for supremacy. One cruiser/carrier was built, which was so large that it was almost a new class to itself.

"Jane's Spaceflight Update - 2029"
Macintosh Publishing, 2029

The initial target for the fleet was the mathematical source of the meteors. This corresponded with a region of space encompassing millions of cubic kilometers, but the fleet needed someplace to start. The fleet moved into formation, and undertook just over two days of constant acceleration before the ships were going the proper speed for the transition. Programming in the jump, the advance fleet activated the FT-Hop drive and thumbed its nose at conventional physics and traveled the tens of millions of kilometers of empty space.

The small advance fleet twisted and snapped out of the dimensions between space in one coordinated motion. The cutters and frigates arrayed in a three dimensional arrowhead around the massive Chinese carrier. The rest of the ships were either guarding the carrier or in the case of the support craft, trailing several thousand kilometers behind the fleet. Active EMS sensors reached out and scanned the void. While the fleet was now in the asteroid belt, the closest dust particles were thousands of kilometers away.

The five million year old dust particles were ignored compared to the flashes of high-energy subatomic particles. Correlating the readings from a multitude of sources the fleet zeroed in on a distant battle.

Adair studied the readouts from the FleetMESH. None of the target ships were of any known energy configurations. They were also all moving at the very edge of speed and maneuverability of the known ships. Their fleet was on a tangent, but the orders would come through momentarily.

"Captain, it is the Dalian - putting Zhong jiang Wei-Ding on." Alphosine didn't wait for Adair to acknowledge before putting the communication through the bridge speakers.

"All ships, this is the Dalian. Launch all fighters and alter course to intercept. Await for a positive id before engaging enemies. Task Force Hammer and Task Force Anvil have also been sent laser tight-beam. Ping acknowledgement."

Adair nodded towards Alphosine. "Please give a ping of acknowledgement." He pressed buttons on his arm controls. "Launch all strike craft. Strike craft are to assume an offensive position at the point of the task force and take targeting information from Dalian fire-control."

He disengaged the comms after hearing the confirmation and then leant forward towards helm. "Match the fleet movements - set course to intercept."

He leant back, and then glanced over at Delilah. "Tell me you have something there. We can't go into this blind."

Delilah peered intensely on her holo displays.

"There appears to be a one-sided battle. One small cutter sized craft is engaging a small fleet of larger cruiser and frigate sized ships. The smaller ship is using some sort of energy based weapon to disable the engines of the larger craft. It's taking a great deal of incoming fire, but does not appear to be taking any significant damage." Delilah paused and then looked back to Adair. "That's the same type and location that we were attacked on the moon. I think we should target that small one - it's clearly superior."

Adair considered a moment, leaning on the arm of his command chair.

"Contact the fleet. Aid the smaller craft - have the fighter craft work to disable any of the other ships trying to flee."

Alphosine acknowledged the instruction and then moved to do it as Delilah frowned.

"I said we should attack the smaller craft."

"We've not seen what the Mara can do, however it's not attacking to destroy but to disable. It's acting like a law enforcement trying to capture. The other ships are returning fire - but their attacks are not getting through."

"Captain?" Alphosine called over as the screen showed the strike craft closing and spreading out to dance in and out of the alien crafts. "I'm getting a direct communication. It's from the Mara."

Delilah scoffed at Adair being correct. Adair tries to give an apologetic look back, and then turns to Alphosine. "Put him on."

He looked up to the main-screen knowing who he expected even as the heavy crested alien came into focus.

"Agriprom Prime Lalrit" Adair grinned. "I was wondering if you could use a hand out here?"

The alien leaned forward, frowning into the image. In the background, the interior of the ship looked like it was organic grown white bone.

"Captain Fox. I warned you not to interfere. This is a Hegemony affair."

"With respect, Agriprom Prime - a hundred million humans would disagree, or they would if they were still alive." Adair stood up and approached the view screen. "Since they you let their voices be taken, we're here to speak for them."

"Captain, the rest of the fleet is breaking off, we are all chasing individual targets."

"Thank you. Agriprom Prime, we have some work. We shall talk soon." He made a throat-cutting motion. Alphosine cut the channel.

"Helm - choose one of the available targets and alter course to intercept. Fire control - You are free to once you have firing solutions. Save torpedoes for direct confirmation. Aim to disable."

The SS Canary Island breaks formation, turning towards an alien cruiser which is three times the size, and easily five or six times the mass. The alien target disengages from the Mara ship, and turns to attack.

"All stations, brace for combat." Adair announces over the channel.

The alien cruiser tracked the beam weapons on the Canary Island. High-energy mesons slammed into the ship, causing atomic decay to the hull superstructure and cutting through the ship in several places.

The impacts could be heard through the ship, however there was no interruption to the gravity or to the power.

"Several hits to the neck - life support, labs and auxiliary fire control and munitions storage." Delilah relayed.

"Secure bulkheads. We also want to drop the gravity down in case we are hit. It will be less impact to the crew."

One of the Chinese offices was manning the operational console gave the acknowledgement. The gravity shifted and throughout the ship bulkheads closed down to protect and isolate the various parts of the ship in case of a catastrophic decompression.

"Return fire. I want a firing solution on the torpedoes." Adair sat back down in his chair, and pulled across the restraints designed to help hold him in his chair.

Outside tiny strike-craft roared trying to strafe the alien cruisers only to be chased off by drones which were even smaller and more agile than the single person crafts. The larger ships continued their spirals and arcs trying to get the upper hand or draw other ships towards positions where two or more ships could fire on them.

Mesons lanced out, leaving venting oxygen when the primary tanks were cut, the damage also managing to damage the failsafes to isolate and divert the remaining oxygen to undamaged stores. Other impacts further aft damaged the coolant system, causing the ship to be required to cut it's power by 40% -slowing down the persuit. The reactors started running dangerously hot while the ship started leaving sparkling array of frozen gases.

Bridge relays overloaded by the sudden shifts in power, and several screens exploded in a shower of sparks. Delilah screamed as she was thrown back from her console, debris and sparks raining down on her.

Adair gripped the side of his chair, the shaking rattling the bracing holding the chair down. "Delilah!" he called out, his finger darting towards the medical bay button.

"I'm good." she hissed back through clenched teeth. She reached across, holding her right arm close to her body. Her uniform was burnt and shredded, and her skin underneath was bubbled and bleeding. "Fix this, Fox!"

Adair punched the button to open up intra-ship communications, "Engineering... I need more manoeuvring. It's coming around behind us - and I can't out-turn it anymore."

"We're in danger of blowing here - I need to take the mains down." Came the reply from the intercom.

"Run us hot. I'll take the chances." Adair replied, and then turned to his helm officer. "Tactical - bring us around to 258.3 mark 28"

"Aye, aye - Captain" Helm acknowledged the command

The Canary Island was slowly losing the battle, and it's precious reactors and HEPE engines would come under fire - which would leave the ship crippled - or worse. It's fighter escorts were being drawn out of position by the drones.

The lights flickered.

"That was the Eapo reactor." Came the call from the engineering deck. The sound of klaxons could be heard.

"Power down by 60%. Hold on, we're almost there." Another explosion rocked the ship, this time gravity spiked and Adair held onto the arm of the chair as two of the bridge officers were launched out of their chairs. Delilah had braced herself to the remains of her console, but screamed out in pain again.

"Now! Drop us down - Bearing 181 - naught." Adair gripped his chair as the ship lurched downward, the gravitics barely able to compensate in time.

The Canary Island suddenly ducked down like a balloon with the air taken out of it. Looming head-on was the Dalian. As Adair's ship passed below the ship, it opened fire. The trap sprung.

The cruiser broke off the attack and turned aside, however it had been damaged by Dalian's volley. The large carrier-cruiser continued towards the next cluster, allowing the Canary Island to turn about and finish disabling the alien craft.

"Fox!" Delilah had limped her way to another terminal, and had strapped herself into the chair. Her right arm was strapped across her breast by the seat restraints, and she remained conscious by sheer will alone. Her left knuckles were white as she gripped the console, "This is a trap. We have most of the initial ships disabled but it cost us two thirds of our strike craft."

Delilah altered the tactical to a wider scan. There was a fresh set of incoming targets. Their energy signature matched that of the alien ships. "We have some fresh incoming opposition - we won't be able to hold them back."

"Captain - incoming from the Mara."

"I was perhaps hasty, Captain Fox, in my criticism of you. It is most fortunate that you are here, however it appears that we will be unable to celebrate this. The D'rak N'li continue jam my communications - I have no means to relay their betrayal to the Hegemony."

Alphosine nodded, "He is correct. I do not understand how. Localized communications are unaffected, however any broadcast messages - even tight-beam laser - are being scattered."

Adair leant forward against his restraints to look at the Mara on the viewscreen with grim determination. "Agriprom Prime Lalrit, This fleet is here to defend our planet and to bring these D'rak N'li to justice. We will hold the line."

The screen went out as another shock rippled through the ship. The reinforcements had entered close combat range.

"Cut all power, and life-support. I want us to appear as drifting. Delilah - passive EMS only." Adair looked down at his command chair, mentally doing some calculations. "Tell me when you see millimeter band distortion. It should be about bearing 223."

Gravity suddenly cut out, along with the primary lights leaving only the dull glow of battle lights. "If I had my way here, I'd change that red. It's so angry." He muttered under his breath. "Delilah - tactical situation update."

"Somewhere between not good and horrible. The Bonn and Panyu are crippled. The Paris has been destroyed - their Eapo reactor went critical and set off its torpedo municans. The Dalian is still fighting, but the opponents are focusing on it. The Mara craft too is almost out of commission." Delilah was leaning over the console and working with one arm.

"Just a bit longer. We can do this." Adair gripped his chair as the gravity flared with the impact of weapons.

"I'm seeing the millimeter fluctuations just where you said." Delilah called out, holding onto her chair as the bridge was tossed. "We have incoming."

Task Force Hammer and Task Force Anvil folded out of the space between space itself. The crippled Earth and Mara forces were joined by fresh ships arriving from opposite sides to cut off any retreat. Immediately the destroyers and cruisers divided and started relieving the pressure caused by the D'rak N'li. The lead ship from Task Force Anvil was the UWSF Hermes which set course to aid the Dalian. Fresh strike-craft were launched while the damaged ships returned to existing carrier craft for repairs and replenishment.

"Engineering, please direct immediate repairs. Keep me apprised once we have are Eapo reactors back online. Flight deck - prepare for damaged incoming crafts." Adair leant back in his chair, exhaling. "Medical - I need staff on the bridge right now. Delilah is hurt."

Delilah looked over, her face was already going pale and blood was dripping down her side. "Like hell. I'm here to the bitter end!"

Outside, the tide of the battle was sliding back towards the Earth forces. Although outgunned and facing superior technology, the Humans were slowly wearing down the combat effectiveness of the alien craft.

While waiting for engineering to get the engines back online, Adair studied the dancing pixel-motes on the holoscreen tracing the various ships. Slowly a pattern inside the chaos appeared to him. He watched a moment longer, to reaffirm his thoughts.

"I think I've found the key ship in the alien fleet. Alphosine, get the word out to our fleet."

She looked back and shook her head. "I'm sorry Sir, when our reinforcements arrive the jamming signal was increased. Interfleet communications is now not reliable."

Adair dropped his fist down on the chair. "Same with our own communications to our fighters, I assume?"

"Affirmative." Alphosine agreed.

"Focus on grid 14 mark 18." The screen shifted to mark one of the alien crafts.

"What? It's no different from any other one." Remarked Fredrico.

Delilah watched the screen, then looked down to her own holos. "Adair - you're brilliant. I can see it." She watched a moment longer, coughing and trying to keep from slouching against the restraints.

"You need to keep track on it - the other ships keep shifting to try to hide their focus."

"Exactly. I think that's the ship we need to take out."

A moment passed. Delilah then stood up, reaching to brace herself on the recessed hand-holds.

"Where the hell do you think you're going?" Adair looked at Delilah.

"We don't have time to argue. We're the only two who can see this - and you are needed to captain the ship. Besides, you're a crappy shuttle pilot." Delilah's tone was affectionate.

"Delilah - you are needed here. Look at those defenders - that is a suicide mission. And you are injured. You should be in sick-bay - not going out there." Adair unclipped his restraints and stood up. "I forbid you to go. That's a direct order!"

Delilah smiled back at Adair. "Direct order - oh that's cute. Hey this way I'll miss my court martial." She slowly looked around the bridge. "Al - take care of him for me."

She floated out the exit, murmuring. "Direct order… and it was his idea to steal the ship."

Adair scowled, and then hit the control panel.

Boyd's voice is heard - klaxons in the back ground.

"Munitions - A-hoy-hoy."

"Boyd!" Adair explained quickly. "Get down to the flight deck. Stop Delilah. She's about to go out on a suicide mission."

"Why did you order that!" Anger crept into Boyd's voice.

"I would never do that. I tried to stop her, but she just ignored me."

There was a pause and a chuckle. "That sounds more like it. Leave it up to me. Munitions out."

Adair looked across the room, and settled on a young cadet who floated near the periphery. "Ensign Campbell, isn't it?" he nodded to the console where Delilah had manned. "Take Operations. I need a situation update."

Ensign Campbell, one of the newly appointed started to float over with her longish dirty blond hair flowing out behind her when gravity flickered back on, sending her to the deck below.

"Eapo is back online. We should be combat ready in minutes." came the voice from Engineering.

Adair gave a sympathetic look as Ensign Campbell picked herself up and manned the station.

"Um, Captain Fox, Sir. We just launched two strike craft."

'Dammit Boyd!' thought Adair. "Alphosine, raise them!"

"Sorry. I cannot. We're still being jammed."

Adair clenched his fists. "Tactical on screen. Okay take us in after them. Fire-control - try to clear any ships which close to engage on our strike craft."

Delilah and Boyd flew the small agile fighters between the larger capital ships and dodged explosions and debris being strewn about. Every time drones were about to get a firing solution, the gunners from the Canary Island would protect the small fighters.

Weapons started to concentrate their fire on the Canary Island. Already battered from the initial battles, the reactors flared before fail-safes engaged to prevent overloading. Lights failed and panels sparked. There was a sudden lurching feeling, and unbeknownst to the crew, the port nacelle was completely severed from the superstructure.

Alphosine suddenly screamed and tossed her headset off her head. The squeal of multichannel communications could be heard suddenly blasting to life. She looked sheepish as she claimed "Communications has been restored."

Overhead the multitude of orders immediately burst to life over the intercom, overlaid each other.

"Al - give me just our Task Force. And recall Delilah and Boyd." Adair assessed the damage on the bridge as debris floated freely and sparks lashed across from blown panels.

"Captain Fox - this is Admiral Rees. You are over-extended and critically damaged - fall back." The other voices silenced and only Admiral Rees came over the intercom.

"Acknowledged Admiral - I was protecting my team. We identified the ship blocking all communications. We are severely crippled. Make sure it counts, Admiral" Adair punched at his command chair to call up engineering, however his chair controls were dead.

"Acknowledge Captain - we salute you." Admiral's reply came over the comm.

"Captain Fox - this is the Devon Wolfe - we will throw everything we have to bring you back." Other ships started to acknowledge and alter their course to intercept and rescue the SS Canary Island.

Another voice cut through the various chatter on the radio.

"Don't worry Fox. I'll make sure that your friends come back." It was Christina Grigg, the tone of her voice conveyed emotion.

As the Canary Island floated crippled several ships formed into a close formation to protect it from any further damage. The SS New York dove past the crippled destroyer to take over escort and protection of the two strike craft piloted by Boyd and Delilah.

Ensign Campbell raised her hand. "Ummm… Sir?"

Adair turned from the Admiral to look at the Operations Ensign. "What do you have for me. Don't be afraid to just call it out."

"Look Sir!"

There were ripples in the fabric of space around them - and ships were starting to emerge. Dozens of ships. Drones started to launch. The fleet was surrounded, and out-numbered.

Adair looked down. The feeling of overwhelming odds - of the simulation. No… life itself… was cheating. A no-win situation. In his mind it was the D'rak N'li reinforcements. In his mind, it had all been for nought.

Alphosine let out a cheer and lunged across the bridge to hug Adair.

"They are Mara! Lalrit must have gotten the word out. We did it! You did it!"

Adair looked up as the fighting slowed - the Mara ships sweeping in to disable those drones still fighting and started to aid the crippled human ships.

"I didn't do anything. I'm not a hero." Adair felt confused. He watched the screen, and then looked down. Boyd was the hero - Delilah was the hero.

Every soldier who put their life on the line was the hero.

Alphosine felt Adair's doubt in his shoulders. She spoke quietly as the bridge sparked and debris floated around them. "It was your plan, Adair. You rallied us together. You sacrificed our ship to allow Delilah and Boyd to succeed. No, you are not a hero. You are a Leader."

12

238,948,283.

That is the estimate of lives lost during the bombardment of Earth. The loss of history and the effects on the development and future of Mankind is almost incalculable.

Even with Hegemony assistance, humanity would take decades to repair the damage, and centuries for the effects will resonate throughout human culture. Humanity had a rough birthing, and now faced a new dawn among the stars.

As a Transitory Member of the Hegemony.

"Becoming One"
Secretary-General Shelley Dione (ret.), UWSF , 2031

Adair reached down to tug-straighten his UWSF dress uniform. He looked back up to himself in the reflection of the interior surface. His eyes had bags under them, and while it was cut in the military fashion, his hair still somehow looked unkempt.

His shoulder had the bars and his collar the pips of the rank of "Commander". In the history of the United World, and the United Nations before it, has never been a Commander so young. On his left breast was also three medals, shiny and gleaming. And there were more countries wanting to honour his deeds.

Adair still did not like being called a hero. In his mind Delilah was the hero. Boyd was the hero. Every pilot who did not come back from the Battle of the Dark (as the encounter was publicised in the media) were the heros.

They all had been given medals - of course. Many pilots were awarded medals posthumous, but thankfully Delilah and Boyd had survived to stand beside him at the various ceremonies when they were touted as the new leaders for a new age.

The door chimed and cycled open. Strange alien walls and fittings which looked like organic-grown bone. No other human ever had the honour of being invited to the Hegemony capital ship stationed in the Kuiper belt.

Adair walked into the inner sanctum of Agriprom Prime Lalrit. The tall Mara sat behind a desk with two other Mara, and beside two other creatures. One looked like a strange collection and mess of bundled sticks and nodules, like a chaotic mess of old-time tinker-toys. The other was a tall bulky creature which looked like it was wearing a thin gauze over-top of armor plating.

"Commander Fox." The Mara spoke English, and small devices around the necks of the others translated.

"I would like to introduce Sui'loo Prime T'hoo'soo of the Hoo'Lou'Loon," the stick-bundle creature gestured, "and X'il Prime Ziq of the Xyquum." The squat bulky creature made a grunting roar.

"These are your closest Hegemony members to your world. Sui'loo Prime T'hoo'soo represents your sponsorship to the Hegemony. While Humanity not met the requirements , it has been granted Transitory Hegemony Constituent status. The interference of the D'rak N'li had caused the Hegemony to grant this."

Adair was silent. It was unusual for the Mara to be forthcoming.

"The Mara will continue to work with Humanity, of course. Your race will be free to set your own course among the stars. You will of course need to negotiate with the Hoo'Lou'Loon, but those will come in time." Agriprom Prime Lalrit did not show any emotion as he spoke, but there was a faint sense of closure. Of an ending, and a new beginning.

"Right now humans need to rebuild the damage. There are not many looking up to the stars." Adair points out.

"There will be. There will be those like you - who will still strive for more. I am not your enemy, Commander Fox. And you have proven you are not mine." Agriprom Prime Lalrit rose and crossed his four arms across his chest in a formal bow.

-- == == --

Adair stepped out of the Tsiolkovsky landing craft on the sand-swept beach. With his future still being determined by the re-established UWSF command, he had taken his personal time to track down Alphosine. This lead him to the small island of 'Uvea.

The local airport on the island was only for small local planes; it was not designed for any space-borne crafts. Adair choose instead to land on a remote unused beach.

As he stepped out, SUVs crossed the beach and drove to where the landing craft came to rest on the beach. Two ornately dressed men stepped out, standing at attention, followed by Alphosine.

She was dressed in a white flowing light dress that bared her midriff. She had what looked like a sash of flowers around her shoulder, and expensive gold earrings and jewellry. Her hair was longer now and done up with colourful flowers.

She ran over, throwing her arms around Adair, embracing him.

"Adair! I didn't believe it when you said you were coming."

"I can't believe you left the space forces." He replied, looking up and down. "Wow… you look so very… just wow."

She beamed. "You do too. I've watched all the news I could about you."

The wind blew, sending Adair's hair blowing.

"I've had something I've been wanting to say."

A sad look fell across Alphosine's eyes as she stepped close, taking Adair's hands.

"I know. And I have something I should have said long ago." Tears welled up into her eyes.

"I don't understand." Adair said. "I've wanted to say that I lo…"

Alphosine lifted up a finger. "Don't. Please."

Teardrops fell down her cheek onto the leafy sash.

"Adair. My father is the Lavelua of this island. I'm betroth. I have been since I was seven." Alphosine regained her resolve, and her face became again pristine and perfect.

Adair felt his heart cracking. "You're…"

"Yes. I guess you would call it a princess. One day I will be Queen. After what happened - they would not let me leave. It's too dangerous. And I need to think of my people - not just what I want." Alphosine explained softly, and with compassionate and patience for Adair.

"But, what do you want?" Adair pleaded.

"It doesn't matter what I want. Adair… I am sorry. I never wanted to hurt you."

She held his hands - keeping her composure with practiced regal charm.

Adair tried to keep her gaze, but he couldn't. His eyes dropped, and he let out a breath that he had been holding.

"I am sorry." Alphosine whispered her voice cracking softly. She felt his hands going limp in hers, and slowly let them drop before backing away.

Adair stood as the jeep left the beach. He turned and walked back into the landing shuttle. He sat down in the back as the ship's AI came to life, "Welcome back Commander. Where would you like to go?"

fin.

Here is a preview of Stefan Budansew's next book, Arktos Falling. Please look forward to this novel to be released later in 2015.

Chapter 1

From a undying plane of limbo came a rush of noise. A cacophony of impulses assaulted cells which had been held in a suspended state between life and death. His body was held in a supposed zero-gravity environment, but something was wrong.

Fire lanced through cacophonic sound and a new series of harsh sounds mixed with the rushing around him. Senses blazed - icy cold and then white hot. Cells rebooting and sending their complaints through his body.

Conscious thoughts pushed through the screaming neurons. *This isn't what it was like back on.. where was I? Who am I?*

There was something familiar to that sound. Not the rush.. the other one. It was the sound of his own voice.. screaming. Not loud..a raspy mummy-like scream from the pit of his soul. He tried to open his eyes - but muscles wouldn't work.

Am I there? Did it work? He forced himself to focus. The rushing noise was subsiding, and he realized that it was the sound of the hibernation crèche being drained. Every nerve fired, every muscle locked and every sense overloaded.

His mind felt like it was as abused as his body. Memories were hazy and flicked back and forth like looking through someone else's photo album. He tried to focus to cut through the sensations.

New sounds were joining the previous ones - twisting confusing symphonies of noise. His brain was not yet ready to process them, and as his body woke, more sensations were flooding in faster than he could process.

Muscles strained and ached, and his eyelids cracked apart. Like a sarcophagus opening, his mind was overloaded by the visual sensations. If there was anything in the dust of his stomach, it would have tried to leap out. *It shouldn't be like this. What happened to the mission? What happened to me?*

He had to force his aching muscles to blink several times to try to focus. The rushing roar was fading, and as his eyes focused, he saw the cryogenic gel; now faded and muted; flowing up and out of the seal which had been opened in his cryogenic crèche. Peeking through the opening, his mind did flip-flops as the material spilt out upwards and sideways, his body was hanging upside down against the ceiling.

He clenched his eyes, and forced his mind to settle. *Is this normal? Is this a dream?* He peeked out again, and as his equilibrium sought a 'floor' it came to the determination that he was hanging upside down. *This is wrong - there shouldn't be gravity. Or there should.. on the floor. And there should be people around.* He opened his mouth to try to talk, but only croaked again.

His ears were assaulted again, and he realized it was a sensation outside his head. Something was talking to him - but not through the computer speakers installed in the cryogenic crèche.

"Observation Human. Your body does not seem to have survived the cryogenic process.. Interrogative Human. Are you still alive?"

The small voice came through the opening from which the gel continued to seep out. He couldn't see the source of the talking.

"Pronouncement Drone. This was a waste of time. We are doomed." There was a strange whistling and whirring noise to answer that.

Mustering all that he could, he put all of his focused energy into screaming a response. From deep inside the now leaking cryogenic crèche, came a faint raspy whisper.

"Alive."

He wasn't yet sure of who he was, but he was not about to be left behind. Feeling every bit the mummy that he looked, the first hour was pure agony. The growing intensity of the gravity against his body as more and more of the gel leaked out made him wish several times for death.

Slowly, burning nerves and muscles came to life, and he felt he could slightly move his arms and legs. *Where are all the others? Where are the drones? What about the 'doc-in-a-box' which was built into each of the crèches?*

When the voice had returned, its source had moved. It was now above his head, coming through the crack from which the gel continued to slowly drain. "Interrogative Human. Are you still alive?"

Still alive? He felt anger and frustration build up. *Of course he was! Where are the doctors? Where was Navya? Where are the other crew?*

"Yes." he managed to croak. "Out"

"Assessment Human. You have the strength of a fried egg on the grill of a semi-truck. You have a 78.4 percent chance of not surviving outside the cryogenic pod."

He considered this. The pain had dulled to a level where it was not consuming all of his consciousness, and he could see and hear reasonably well. His memories still flitted back like a shadowy mixture of someone else's flickr account. Old videos and images mixed with strangers and unfamiliar places. "I've survived already. Let me out." he croaked back.

"Acknowledgement."

ABOUT THE AUTHOR

Stefan Budansew has been a fan of science fiction for decades and has worked on the background for Immersion for years before putting it to paper. He lives in Toronto, Ontario, with his wife Belinda and brother Nathan and cat.

This is his first novel.

Made in the USA
Charleston, SC
22 September 2015